A Game of Murder

By the same author

Death and Deception

A Game of Murder

Ray Alan

ROBERT HALE · LONDON

© Ray Alan 2008
First published in Great Britain 2008

ISBN 978-0-7090-8650-5

Robert Hale Limited
Clerkenwell House
Clerkenwell Green
London EC1R 0HT

www.halebooks.com

The right of Ray Alan
to be identified as author of this work has been
asserted by him in accordance with the
Copyright, Designs and Patents Act 1988

2 4 6 8 10 9 7 5 3 1

Typeset in 11/15.5pt New Century Schoolbook
Printed and bound in Great Britain by
Biddles Limited, King's Lynn

CHAPTER ONE

Detective Sergeant Dick Marsh had only been attached to the Chelsea police station in London for a few weeks. He was at his desk finishing a case report when Superintendent Lamb walked into the office. 'Inspector Forward about?' he asked.

'No, sir. He's gone to church,' replied Marsh.

'Church!' exclaimed the superintendent. 'What's he gone to church for? Ask forgiveness for his sins?'

'No, sir.' Marsh smiled. 'He's gone to see Father O'Connor to find out how Terry Kennedy is getting on.'

'Oh. Still trying to help that young tearaway, is he? Well when he gets back, tell him I want to see him.'

'Right, sir. He shouldn't be long.'

Marsh watched the superintendent leave and carried on tidying up his report. He finally put it in an envelope and placed it on top of Detective Inspector Forward's desk. As he walked back to his own desk, the phone rang. He sat down and answered it. 'Detective Sergeant Marsh ... Oh, hello, sir. Superintendent Lamb was just here. He wants to see you when you get back ... No idea. That's all he said ... OK. See you soon then.'

Marsh hung up and was debating whether to go for a coffee when the door opened and a man he hadn't seen before walked in. He was in his mid to late fifties, with a broad smile that matched his large frame.

'Hello. You must be DS Marsh,' he said. Offering his hand, he introduced himself. 'Dave Norris. Drug squad.'

The two men shook hands.

'I've heard about you from my governor,' said Marsh.

'Lies. All lies,' said Norris, grinning. 'Not going to keep you. But as I was passing through I just wanted to say hello and see how you're getting on with my old mate, Bill Forward. Is he about?'

'No, he's out at the moment. We're getting along fine. Mind you, his offbeat sense of humour takes some getting used to.'

Dave Norris laughed. 'I know what you mean. But he's a bloody good copper. You can learn a lot from him. We were rookies at Hendon together. He's a loyal friend when you need one. When you get to know him better you'll discover that.' Dave Norris looked at his watch. 'Better go. My governor isn't as understanding as yours. See you around. Perhaps we'll have a drink together next time I'm this way. Tell Bill I popped in and said hello.'

'I will.' Marsh smiled to himself as the big man left. He could imagine what the two men got up to when they were rookies together. Noticing some box files that were lying in a pile on a shelf beside his governor's desk, he decided to straighten them up and put them neatly in alphabetical order.

On his way back to Chelsea police station, Bill Forward was wondering what Superintendent Lamb wanted to see him about. He was pleased with his meeting with Father O'Connor and the way he was keeping Terry Kennedy under his wing and out of trouble. Although not a Catholic himself, Bill Forward admired the way the father had run his youth club. And he was grateful for the way he arranged the meetings between Kennedy and himself. The lad had proved to be a very reliable informant, without whose help Bill Forward might not have got local villain Mark Tucker arrested and put away for twelve years. He knew that Father O'Connor could be trusted to keep the relationship between Kennedy and the inspector strictly to himself.

Although Chelsea was one of London's busiest police stations, Bill Forward had a regular space in the car park. He drove in, parked and went straight to his office, to find it much tidier than when he left.

'Have you had a woman in here, Marsh?' he asked as he looked round. 'Not that little Irish PC that you fancy, was it?'

'I had a bit of a tidy up, that's all,' said Marsh, ignoring the sarcasm.

Bill Forward sat at his desk and, running his finger over the top, said, 'Missed a bit here but never mind. You'll make someone a lovely wife one day.' He picked up the envelope containing the case report. 'What's this?'

'The report on the Tucker case. It's right up to date now. How did you get on with the Kennedy boy?'

Bill Forward looked at the Tucker report as he said, 'Fine. Young Kennedy is doing all right. Father O'Connor seems to have him well on the road to becoming a decent citizen again. We'll just have to keep our fingers crossed.' He read through the case report and gave a nod of approval. 'Good work, sunshine. Get another copy done and I'll take it to the super.'

Marsh picked up a copy of the papers from his desk and held them up with a look of innocence. 'Like these, you mean?'

Bill Forward made no comment but smiled to himself as he took the papers from his twenty-four-year-old sergeant and left.

*

Superintendent Lamb was standing at the window of his office when Bill Forward knocked and entered.

'Come in, Forward. Close the door.'

The inspector walked over and handed the case file to Lamb. 'Here's the final report on the Tucker case, sir. Marsh has done a good job on it.'

The superintendent took the file and put it on his desk. 'I'll read it later. How are you and Marsh getting on?'

'He's coming along fine. We've only been together for eight weeks but I like him. He's very efficient and quick to learn.'

'That's good. He's still sewing his wild oats, I believe?'

Bill Forward smiled. 'I haven't poked my nose in that direction, so far.'

Lamb grinned and nodded as he said, 'Well, when he knows you better he'll no doubt discuss his private life with you. Now, sit down and tell me about your visit to church this morning. What was all that about?'

Bill Forward sat facing the desk. 'I promised young Kennedy's mother that I'd keep an eye on him. I went over to see him and make sure he was behaving himself, which he is. Father O'Connor finds him a great help with the other lads in the youth club. He sets a good example, according to the father.'

'There's a turn up for the book. A Kennedy setting a good example! Wonders will never cease if that little tearaway goes straight. His father was rotten to the core and the lad will probably go the same way. So why do you bother?'

'I bother because I don't want to see Terry go the same way as his old man. Yes, he was a bad lot and caused his family more grief than they deserved. But Bob Kennedy died in a prison hospital. A prison I helped to put him in. Terry was only twelve and his mother was terrified he would get in with a bad lot and end up like his father. She never held it against me that I was the arresting officer when we caught her husband. The truth is, she was glad he was locked up and was only concerned for her son. When she knew she had cancer and hadn't got long to live, she made me promise to keep an eye on him, and since she died last year I have.'

Superintendent Lamb listened with interest. 'I had no idea the mother had died as well.'

'Yes. So I feel somewhat responsible for helping to keep the boy out of trouble.'

'Yes, I can understand that now. I know he's involved with the priest's youth club, but where does he live now that his mother's gone?'

'With his mother's sister and her husband. Not far from the youth club. He's well looked after there. And they've got an eighteen-year-old son, so the boys are company for each other.'

'Right. Now getting back to the Tucker case. When did you first realize it was him that was setting up the warehouse job?'

Bill Forward smiled. 'I had a reliable informant who gave me date, time and which of the local villains were involved. We had the perfect set-up to get them. And we did. Just as they were loading the vans.'

The superintendent nodded, but hesitated before saying, 'So your informant was in with them, was he? Must have been, to be able to give you that information.'

'Let's just say, I was lucky. And if you expect me to divulge the name of my informant, I'm afraid I shall disappoint you, sir. You know the rule. Never let anyone know who your informant is. Not only for their own safety, but in case we need them again.'

'Yes, of course. Well, once again congratulations on getting Tucker put away.' He stood up and walked to the door with

Bill Forward following him. 'And good luck with young Kennedy. I hope he doesn't let you down.'

'Thank you, sir. I hope so too.'

Lamb saw Bill Forward out. He was curious as to who that informant was.

CHAPTER TWO

Stafford House was situated at the far corner of Chart Gardens, an exclusive cul-de-sac within walking distance of the fashionable Kings Road, Chelsea. The impressive six-bedroom house was concealed by a high wall and a mixture of trees protruding from the grounds, giving the impression of a property possessing more land than there actually was. The occupants were Sir Reginald and Lady Pace-Warren. He was in his mid fifties and a successful man in the property business. His very attractive wife was a lot younger than her husband and enjoyed the lifestyle his money had given her. With her husband away on business so much, and feeling depressed, she phoned her friend, Sara Wilson.

'Hello, Sara. It's Fiona.'

'Hello. How are you?'

'Bored with these dark winter nights and fed up with watching these awful television programmes.'

'I know exactly what you mean. It's the one time of the year that I envy those people who can go off to Spain for the winter. David says I can go any time I want to, but I wouldn't really enjoy it without him and he can only take two breaks a year as you know.'

'That's what you get for marrying a doctor, darling. But

Reggie's away a lot too. He's somewhere up north at the moment. He hopes to be back by Friday but isn't sure. Anyway, my reason for ringing is this. I thought I might invite some friends round this Saturday for a buffet dinner. How does that idea grab you?'

'Great. We aren't doing anything and David hasn't got a surgery. I'll check it with him when he gets in, but I'm sure it will be OK.'

'Good. I'll just invite a few couples who I know will get on. When we get bored with conversation I thought we might have some party games.'

'Good idea. But if we play sardines, I'm not getting in a cupboard with Harry Cooper. Cooper the groper we used to call him at school, remember?' she chuckled.

'Ooh, yes,' Fiona giggled. 'Well, I promise I shan't be inviting that great lump. I'll make sure all the men are worth getting squeezed in the cupboard with.' She laughed.

'Oh, hang on a minute. David has just walked in. It's Fiona, darling. She wants to know if we can go over on Saturday for a buffet dinner and a few laughs. He's just nodded and given the thumbs-up, so we're on. What time?'

'Between seven and seven thirty?'

'Lovely. See you then. Bye.'

Fiona was happy as she hung up, and looking forward to inviting her other guests and arranging the evening. And to make sure it was a success, she began making a list of party games. There was one in particular that she wanted to include and that was the murder game.

The taxi pulled up at the entrance to the MacCann hotel in Newcastle. Sir Reginald Pace-Warren paid the driver and walked into the reception, where he checked into a double-bedded room that had been booked for one night under the

name of Carrington. He took the key from the pretty receptionist and smiled.

'My wife is doing some shopping, so she'll be along later.'

'Newcastle is a great shopping place, sir,' the girl said.

'As long as she doesn't spend all my money, I don't mind,'
he joked.

Carrying his small suitcase into the lift, he pressed the
button for the second floor. Room 48 was a comfortable en-
suite double bedroom with two armchairs each side of a coffee
table. He sat on the bed and tested the mattress. Then, taking
his wash bag from the suitcase, he went to the bathroom to
freshen up. When he went back into the room he sat in an
armchair and looked at his watch. It was almost 5.15 p.m.
and he knew he wouldn't have to wait long for his visitor.
After looking at some business papers and checking the
details, the telephone rang. He picked up the receiver and
was pleased when he heard a warm sexy voice say, 'Hello.'

'Hello, darling. Where are you?' he asked quietly.

'Just a few minutes from the hotel. I'll be with you soon.'

'I don't think I can wait that long.'

'Feeling that randy, are you? I'll have to think of a way to
relax you, won't I?'

'Yes, please.' His voice sounded slightly breathless.

'Well, save your strength till I get there,' she said, then
asked, 'What's the bed like?'

'Perfect.' He smiled. 'Just get here and you can find out for
yourself. By the way. It's room forty-eight and the young
receptionist thinks you've been shopping. Just in case she
speaks and mentions it.'

'OK. My taxi is just pulling up outside now. See you in a
minute.'

*

It was just after 5.30 p.m. and Bill Forward and Dick Marsh were about to go home when the internal telephone rang. Bill Forward quickly answered it.

'DI Forward.'

'It's Sergeant Cooper, sir. We've got a young man here at the front desk who has just collapsed. He turned up in a right state and asked for you. We've called an ambulance.'

'I'll be right down.' Bill Forward turned to his sergeant. 'Better come with me. It could be an emergency.' Both men hurried out of the office.

When they arrived at the front desk, Sergeant Cooper took them to an interview room.

'We put him in here out of the way, sir,' said Sergeant Cooper, opening the door. 'Constable Barker's with him.'

Bill Forward went in and looked at the young man lying on the table. He had obviously taken a beating about the face and was barely conscious. But despite his appearance, Inspector Forward recognized the young man as Terry Kennedy. Taking the boy's hand, he said, 'Hold on, lad. The ambulance is on its way.

The boy opened his eyes and gave a weak smile of recognition.

'What happened, lad? Who did this to you?'

Before he could answer, the boy passed out, just as the ambulance arrived. The paramedics administered first aid and rushed him to Chelsea and Westminster hospital.

Bill Forward hurried to his office, with Dick Marsh following him.

'Who was that?' Marsh asked.

'That, Sergeant, was Terry Kennedy. Poor little bastard has taken a right beating. I've got to ring Father O'Connor. Then I'll get to the hospital. Once I know his medical condition I'll get over to his aunt and let her know.' He picked up his phone and dialled. He waited a while then replaced the receiver. 'There's no reply. The father's probably at the youth club. You can get along home, Sergeant. I doubt I'll need you any more tonight.'

'Are you sure, sir?'

'Yes, go on. If I need you I'll get you on the mobile.'

'All right. I'll see you in the morning.'

As the two men left the office and went to their cars, the inspector was looking very concerned.

CHAPTER THREE

Ken Morris and Paul Robson had finished their game of golf and were in the clubhouse bar quenching their thirst.

'Looking forward to the dinner party on Saturday?' asked Paul.

'What I'm looking forward to is seeing the lovely Fiona.' Ken grinned.

'I just hope she wears something that gives me a good view of her legs,' said Paul. 'They really are gorgeous. Far too lovely for that man she's married to. What the hell did she ever see in him?'

'I think it's called money. And don't forget the title,' Ken reminded him. 'But I agree with you. She has got gorgeous legs.' He gave a grin as he added, 'I know that most men would like to get under the sheets with her. But remember, you're a married man and mustn't harbour such thoughts.'

Paul laughed as he said, 'Do you think I could play strip poker with her on Saturday?'

Ken chuckled. 'Do you think we could talk about something other than Fiona? The thought of her stripped is making me feel randy. I think a cold drink is required.'

He ordered a fresh round of lager.

*

Andrew Davis, a good-looking man in his early thirties, was sitting in his study when the phone rang. He picked up the receiver. 'Davis speaking.'

'Hello, Andrew. It's Philippa,' said the excited voice.

Philippa Pane was the last person he wanted to talk to. Known for her scandal-mongering, he tried to get rid of her as quickly as possible.

'Hello, Philippa. Janet isn't here, I'm afraid. Perhaps you can ring back later.'

'Have you had an invitation to Fiona's on Saturday?' she enquired.

'Yes, we have.'

'So have I. I wonder if Reggie will dare to show his face? Do you think he will?'

Andrew was completely puzzled by her question. 'Why on earth wouldn't he?'

'Well, haven't you heard?'

'Heard what?'

'About his having a bit on the side. I thought everyone knew. That's why he's away so much apparently. You know what they say, while the mice are away.'

Andrew was getting impatient with her. 'It's while the cat's away, Philippa. And I couldn't care less whether Reggie is having a bit on the side or on the ceiling. It's none of my business. And I'd be careful spreading a rumour like that if I were you. Reggie is a powerful man and could have you in court. Now, if you'll excuse me, I've got work to do.' He hung up and went to the living room, where his wife Janet was reading the daily paper. 'I shouldn't have answered that call.'

'Who was it?' asked Janet.

'That bloody Philippa Pane.'

'What did she want?'

'It appears she is going to the Pace-Warrens' on Saturday.'

'Really? I wonder which man she'll arrive with? Well, at least it's never dull with Philippa around.'

'Wait till you hear her latest bit of scandal.'

'Oh. What is it this time?'

'Did I think it was true that Reggie is having a bit on the side?'

Janet put down her newspaper and smiled. 'Oh dear. So she's heard about that too. Now the whole world will know. Poor Reggie could be in for a rough time at home, I think.'

Andrew looked surprised as he asked, 'You mean you knew about this rumour?'

'Darling, we girls have known for a long time that he probably had a bit of spare somewhere. After all, he is away a lot. And with all that money of his he's very attractive to some women. Don't tell me you men didn't suspect something was going on.'

'I swear I've never heard any man say that about him. Now if you said that Fiona was playing away from home, I could understand it. After all, she's a bloody attractive woman. But who would fancy Reggie, money or no money?'

Janet suddenly became thoughtful. 'Do you think Fiona *has* got a man hidden away somewhere? I know all you men fancy her, but do you think she has? Got a man, I mean.'

Andrew smiled to himself as he started to leave the room. 'You can ask her yourself on Saturday, my love. I've got work to do. See you later.'

Janet picked up the paper but found it hard to concentrate as she had other things on her mind. She was thinking that Saturday might become very embarrassing for someone.

It was just after 7 p.m. on Friday when Father O'Connor returned home from visiting the club and the hospital. He was going to phone Inspector Forward and let him know

Terry Kennedy's condition, as he had promised. But something he had learnt from one of the boys at the club was also troubling him. He dialled the inspector's home number and heard the voice of Jane Forward answer.

'Hello, Mrs Forward. It's Father O'Connor here.'

'Oh, good evening, Father. I take it you want my husband?'

'If it's convenient. I'm not interrupting your meal, am I?'

'No. We're going out for dinner tonight. We want to try the new Italian that's just opened up the road. Just a minute, I'll give him a shout.'

Bill Forward was just out of the shower and getting dressed. He picked up the extension in the bedroom and was apprehensive as he spoke.

'Hello, Father. Has something happened to Terry?'

'He's still in a coma, I'm afraid. The doctor allowed me to see him for a brief moment, and I said a prayer. His aunt had sat with him for a while this afternoon. She held his hand and spoke to him but got no response. She'll be with him again tomorrow.'

'Well, thanks for keeping me up to date. As you know, they won't let us near him at the moment. Frightened that the presence of a policeman might make his condition worse,' he said with anger in his voice. 'The lad trusted me. He might respond to my being there with him. But the medical boys won't budge, so I might have to use my official rank.'

Father O'Connor tried to pacify him. 'Don't fret yourself, Inspector. They have promised to contact you if there is any change in the boy. And I would certainly be in touch the minute I heard anything. Now you and your lovely wife go and enjoy a nice meal and a bottle of red wine. The house red is delightful.' Then quickly added with a chuckle, 'So I'm told.'

Bill Forward managed a smile and was calmer as he said,

'I didn't think there was a wine in existence that you hadn't tried, Father.'

The two men said their goodbyes and the phone call ended without the priest mentioning the other thing that was troubling him. He decided that any news of Tony Farrow being seen in the neighbourhood could wait until tomorrow. He felt that Jane Forward deserved a nice evening meal, without her husband rushing away on police work.

The restaurant was busy and when the Forwards arrived they were glad they'd booked. They were shown to a nice table for two and given the menu and a wine list, which Bill looked at first.

'Father O'Connor said the house red is good.'

Jane was surprised as she asked, 'How can he afford to eat here? I thought priests were poor.'

'He probably comes and samples it for them, to see if it's worth blessing.' Bill grinned. 'No. He said he'd heard it was good. I'm not really familiar with Italian wines and that's all they have here.'

'Why don't we see what we're having to eat first? If we choose fish we won't want red, will we?'

'Point taken.'

They both studied their menus. While they were doing so, a young couple were shown to a nearby table and Bill Forward noticed them. The woman was in her twenties and the man a bit older. He diverted his eyes back to the menu but was trying to put a name to the woman and remember where he had seen her before.

'I've decided what I want,' Jane said.

'What's that?' her husband enquired.

'I shall start with the minestrone and for my main course I'll have the chicken *al limone*.'

'Good choice,' said Bill. 'I shall have the same. And a bottle of the house red. I think we should see if Father O'Connor is right, don't you?' He smiled.

Suddenly he remembered the name of the young woman and wondered who Mandy Lucas was with and whether she was up to her old tricks again.

CHAPTER FOUR

Fiona was delighted that all her guests had accepted her invitation to tomorrow's buffet dinner party. It was something she had wanted to do for quite a while and as she sat looking at her list of guests, she knew they would all enjoy the evening she'd lined up. She had a reputation for giving great dinner parties and was really determined to make this one special. Fiona wanted this get-together to be one they would remember.

As she put her guest list in the drawer of her writing desk, the telephone rang. She answered it and heard Philippa Pane's voice.

'Hello, Fiona. It's Philippa. I'm ringing about tomorrow night.'

'Don't tell me you can't come.'

'Oh, I'll be there. Unfortunately Robert Conway, the gentleman friend I wanted to bring, can't make it. But I think you'll like my new escort,' she said teasingly.

'Is it anyone I know?'

'You could say that. It's Edward King. He fancied you like mad. Remember?'

'The tall skinny boy?' Fiona giggled. 'Good Lord. Fancy him turning up after all these years!'

'Yes. But he's not skinny now. He's quite a hunk actually. Only he's in town visiting friends and I thought it would be nice for you two to meet up again. He's free tomorrow night. So shall I bring him?'

'Please do. I can't wait to see him again, especially if he's a hunk,' laughed Fiona.

'Great. Imagine the faces on the other guests when they see me arrive with a good-looking male companion instead of Robert. They won't know what's hit them.'

'Probably not,' said Fiona, trying to suppress a laugh. 'Look forward to seeing you both tomorrow then. Bye for now.' She hung up, finding it hard to believe that the plump, middle-aged Philippa had managed to snare a good-looking man to go out with her. Or was he only coming to see Fiona, the girl he once fancied like mad and was now *Lady* Fiona? She sat back with a smile, feeling that tomorrow night could be more interesting than she'd planned.

Philippa Pane was pleased with herself and quickly telephoned Edward King on his mobile. She couldn't wait to tell him how excited Fiona was to see him again, and how she hoped he would still find her attractive. Philippa enjoyed exaggerating Fiona's reaction to hearing that Edward would be at the party and enjoyed stimulating him sexually. She wanted to see Edward make a play for Fiona, especially if Reggie was there. The situation appealed to her wicked sense of humour.

Philippa knew that the other women thought of her as being dull and sex-starved. But she didn't always need a man to thrill and excite her. When Robert Conway wasn't available to go to bed with her, she had her pornographic videos and sex toys to give her pleasure.

*

Bill Forward was on his way back to the office in heavy traffic when his personal mobile phone rang. He had it on hands-free and pushed a key to hear Father O'Connor's slightly distorted voice.

'Hello, Inspector. Can you hear me?'

'You're a bit crackly but yes, just about.'

'I thought you'd like to know that the notorious Tony Farrow is in town. Kevin, one of my boys at the youth club, saw him with that girl, Mandy Lucas, and wondered if it was Farrow that might have attacked Terry.'

'I saw her with a man at the Italian restaurant. I wonder if that was him. I'll get Dick Marsh to get his photograph from records and check it out. Thank you, Father. No news on Terry?'

'There's been no change in his condition since yesterday, I'm afraid. I'll call you later. You keep fading on me.'

Back in his office, DI Forward studied the mugshot that Sergeant Marsh brought up from records. 'No doubt about it. This is the man I saw Mandy Lucas with,' he said. 'So this is Tony Farrow. If only I could get Terry to look at this photo and see if it's the man that beat him up!'

Dick Marsh nodded in agreement. 'According to his record, he's a tough bugger. Ex SAS, so he knows how to beat someone up without actually killing them. And it was his obsession with violence that got him discharged from the army. He's worked as a bouncer at several clubs. Been body-guard to various celebrities and has had three aliases that we know of.'

Bill Forward gave a despondent sigh. 'If only Terry would regain consciousness.' He jumped up from his chair and put his coat on. 'I don't care what the medical boys say. I've got to see if there's a chance, even the slightest chance.'

'They'll only refuse to let you near the lad. You know that.'

'In that case, I shall warn them about the seriousness of refusing to assist the police in the course of their enquiries. Get your coat on. I'll need you there as a witness.'

Bill Forward was losing his patience and left the office more determined than ever to see Terry Kennedy.

When he arrived at the hospital, the inspector showed his warrant card and, using his official voice, explained his reason for being there. The nurse at the reception desk picked up her phone and called the duty doctor.

'My sergeant and I need to see Terry Kennedy,' he told the doctor. Holding up his hand to prevent any protest, he quickly added, 'I know the lad is not allowed visitors, apart from Father O'Connor, but this is an official police investigation and we need to see the boy's condition for ourselves. It could be a matter of life and death.'

The young doctor was lost for words, and before he could say anything, Bill Forward said, 'You will be with us, of course, and you have my word we only wish to satisfy ourselves that he is unable to assist us in our enquiries. At the moment, that is.'

The doctor hesitated and then indicated for them to follow him, explaining as they went, 'A nurse checks him every few minutes and he has shown no improvement so far.'

Bill Forward gave an understanding nod and they finally reached Terry Kennedy's room. As they entered they could see that he was wired to two machines that quietly gave a regular bleep. One was connected to his heart and the other to his head. Without hesitation, Bill Forward drew up a chair and sat beside the bed. In a quiet, friendly voice, he said, 'It's Mr Forward, Terry.' Taking the boy's hand, he said, 'If you can hear me, just give my hand a slight squeeze.' There was no immediate response. Bill Forward waited for a moment and was about to give up when Terry's mouth twitched and slowly gave a weak smile. The doctor was surprised and looked at the monitor, which showed an increase in heartbeat. Suddenly, Terry managed to give a gentle squeeze to Bill Forward's finger. The doctor signalled that they should leave and as Bill Forward got up, he whispered, 'You rest now, lad. I shall be back tomorrow.'

He thanked the doctor for letting him see the boy and left.

Driving back to the office, Dick Marsh sat in the passenger seat and grinned.

'Is something amusing you, Marsh?'

'For a minute back there, I think the doctor wondered how you got the boy to respond when the medical lot couldn't. They might invite you to join the staff. I think you'd look nice in a white coat.'

Bill Forward smiled. 'I must say I was bloody glad to see the lad manage a slight smile. If only he could identify it was Farrow who beat him up we could put that bugger behind bars, where he belongs.'

'You'll have to take it easy with the boy, sir, especially with a doctor breathing down your neck,' Marsh said.

'I know. I know. I can't wait to tell Father O'Connor about our visit. No doubt he'll claim it's the power of prayer that worked, rather than my natural bedside manner.'

Bill Forward was pleased with himself and back in his office he telephoned Father O'Connor and told him of his hospital visit. He put the phone down with the hope that tomorrow would prove to be a more successful day.

It was eleven o'clock the following morning when DI Forward arrived at the hospital. He wanted to allow time for the nurses to get patients prepared for their visitors and for Father O'Connor to join him after his regular Saturday morning meeting with his boys at the youth club. After a brief moment with the duty doctor, they all went to Terry Kennedy's room.

Terry appeared to be asleep but the heart monitor showed his heartbeat to have slowed. A nurse was called and she and the doctor hurriedly ushered the two visitors out of the room. There was some activity with a second nurse arriving and Bill Forward waited anxiously for word of the boy's condition.

'I don't understand it,' he said. 'I was convinced he was on the mend when I left him yesterday.'

The priest nodded. 'These things happen. We must hope that it's just a slight setback.'

After waiting for almost an hour, the doctor informed Bill Forward that he would not be able to see Terry today. He left Father O'Connor at the hospital saying a prayer, and went home feeling very despondent.

Fiona was checking last-minute details when she heard a car. Looking at her watch, she wondered who could be arriving so early and called for her housekeeper, Mrs Romaine, to see who it was. She soon heard the voice of her husband and walked from the dining room to greet him.

'Reggie! I'm so glad you've arrived. I began to think you might not make it.'

Sir Reginald gave her a light kiss on the cheek. Then looking at the buffet, said, 'God, there's enough food here to feed an army! When are they due to arrive?'

'Soon. So go and get changed and we'll have a drink,' she said. 'I had hoped you would be here earlier.'

'I'll have the drink and *then* get changed,' he said, pouring himself a glass of whisky. 'I would have been home earlier but

I had an important meeting to attend last night.' He finished his drink and poured another. 'I'll take this one with me. I hope these people are bringing their own bottles! If I remember your buffet and games parties, they cost me a bloody fortune in booze. I wonder what this little lot will cost? After I've had some food I shall go to the study and get some papers sorted out. So I don't want to be disturbed. Get Mrs Romaine to light a fire for me.'

As he walked away, Fiona wondered why he was always so unpleasant when she invited friends round. But she was glad Reggie would be in his study when the others arrived. And hoped he would stay there until the games were over. As long as he was out of the way, it would make things a lot easier for her. And she didn't want her plans spoilt by him making things difficult.

CHAPTER FIVE

With the party well underway, and the games proving a success and entertaining everyone, Fiona was asked when they were going to play the murder game, which many of them were looking forward to.

'Haven't played that for years,' said Janet Davis, with a giggle.

'Me neither,' laughed Angie Morris. 'I remember Ken being the murderer once and he decided to do away with my mother. She didn't see the funny side of it though.'

'Sheila and I went to a murder weekend at a hotel once,' said Paul Robson. 'The murderer turned out to be a woman in her sixties who'd shot her toyboy because he'd had an affair with her daughter.' He laughed. 'I must say it was acted out very well, wasn't it love?'

'It fooled us,' said Sheila. 'We were convinced it was a poor little man with a limp.'

Fiona was enjoying the good-natured atmosphere and offered a pack of prepared cards to everyone, explaining the rules as she did so.

'As you take your card, remember not to let anyone see what you have chosen. After you have seen it, place it face down in the box on the table. Whoever has the jack of clubs is the murderer and mustn't let anyone know. The person with the ace of diamonds is the detective and must wait in the downstairs cloakroom until they hear the victim scream. Then they can carry out their investigation and try to discover who the murderer is.'

The excitement was building as each one took a card.

'Can we use the whole house?' asked Philippa.

'You can hide anywhere except Reggie's study. He's got some papers to go through and he'll give me hell if he's disturbed. Don't forget to keep all the lights out until the detective puts them on as he or she investigates.' Fiona smiled. 'Right, get hiding. And remember, only the murderer can lie as to where they were at the time of the murder. Everyone else must tell the truth.'

Philippa led Edward to Fiona. 'You'd better show Edward where the rooms are. He doesn't know the layout here. Hold her hand, Edward. Then you won't get lost.' She grinned as she left them.

Gradually the lights all over the house went out, leaving only the study with a light on.

'Come on. I'll take you upstairs,' Fiona said quietly to Edward.

'I would love to accept your invitation,' he said, squeezing her hand, 'but apparently I'm not allowed upstairs. You could take me to the cloakroom, though,' he whispered.

'So *you're* the detective! Well, come on. I'll show you the way.'

She took him to the cloakroom by the front door and they went in. He closed the door behind them. It was a small room with little space to move, due to coats hanging along one wall.

'Sorry it's such a tight squeeze,' she said, switching the light on.

'I liked it better with the light off,' he said, putting his hand to her waist and pulling her closer. 'You're even more beautiful than I remember. And reviving old feelings too.'

'If my husband caught us in here like this, we'd be in trouble. I think I'd better leave before things get out of hand.' She pulled herself free and went to leave when she heard the kitchen door open and Mrs Romaine's footsteps cross the hall. Fiona held a finger to her lips for Edward to keep silent. After a few moments, the silence was broken by a woman screaming. 'OK Mr Detective. I'll put the hall lights on and you can prepare to interrogate your suspects,' said Fiona.

Glad to avoid what could have been an embarrassing moment, Fiona opened the door and saw her housekeeper looking pale outside the study door.

'What's the matter?' she asked anxiously.

'It's Sir Reginald. I think he's dead, my lady.'

Fiona hurried to the study and saw her husband's head, resting sideways on the desk where it had fallen, his eyes fixed in a glassy stare. She shook his shoulders and called his name in a desperate effort to revive him. 'Reggie! Reggie. Oh my God! Fetch Doctor Wilson, quickly.'

Edward went to see what the fuss was about. When he saw her husband, he quickly put his arm around Fiona and led her away from the study to a chair in the hall. 'Sit down. I'll get you a drink.'

Fiona sat staring at the floor in disbelief as Edward went. David Wilson hurried downstairs ahead of the others. He looked into the study and went to check Reggie's pulse but there was no sign of life. He then asked Ken Morris to get everyone into the sitting room and keep them away from the study. He saw Edward return and give Fiona a glass of brandy. He nodded approval and asked Edward to help him take Fiona to her bedroom on the first floor. 'Have the police been called?' David asked her.

Fiona shook her head and whispered, 'No.'

The call from Bill Forward to Sergeant Marsh was brief and to the point.

'Send whoever you've got sitting on your lap back to her mother, and get your arse over to Stafford House in Chart Gardens. Someone appears to have killed Sir Reginald Pace-Warren.'

'The property magnet?'

'The very same.'

'Christ! What happened?'

'It appears his guests were playing a game of murder, when someone decided to do the real thing. If you're there before me, your contact is a Doctor David Wilson. Make sure no one leaves. The scenes of crime officer and the forensic team will be on their way.'

'Right. I should be there in ten minutes,' said Marsh. Then he quickly went to the bathroom, cleaned his teeth and gargled with mouthwash to hide the smell of wine on his breath.

There was only one topic of conversation at Stafford House, with all the guests looking at each other in disbelief at what had happened. David Wilson had asked them to remain in the sitting room until the police arrived. He got a sedative from his bag in the car and joined his wife, who was sitting with Fiona in the bedroom, trying to comfort her. Lady Pace-Warren was silent, in a state of shock. Doctor Wilson got a glass of water from the en-suite bathroom and gave it to her with a capsule. Without any resistance, she took the sedative and stared at the floor. After a moment she said quietly, 'Oh God. Who could have done such a thing?'

'You lie down and rest,' said David kindly. 'Sara will stay with you while I go and see the police when they get here.'

Fiona nodded and put her head back on the pillow. David left them and made his way down the stairs. He was giving the others a report on Fiona's condition when the front door-bell rang.

Mrs Romaine opened the door for the scenes of crime officer. After seeing the body in the study, he went to the front door and signalled his team to come in. He asked the house-keeper how many people were in the house and was told twelve. He went to the sitting room and asked everyone to remain there until someone from CID arrived.

By the time Dick Marsh got there, the forensic team were in their protective clothing and examining the study and the garden. He was met by the housekeeper and taken directly to Doctor Wilson, who explained the situation in detail. Marsh asked them both to remain in the sitting room while he questioned the guests as to where they were at the time of the murder. Making notes as he did so.

A few minutes later, Bill Forward arrived. He and Marsh were given protective clothing to wear.

'What have we got?' asked the inspector.

'The housekeeper found him. Doctor Wilson, a guest, pronounced him dead. As you know, it was him that phoned us.'

'Where's the housekeeper now?'

'In the sitting room. Lady Pace-Warren is in her bedroom. The doctor gave her a sedative. Doctor Wilson's wife is with her.'

'And Doctor Wilson?'

'He's in the sitting room with the others.'

'How many people are in the house?'

'Twelve, including her ladyship and the housekeeper. All couples except two. They are ...' He checked his notes. 'Philippa Pane and Edward King. Two women constables are on their way in case we need them with the ladies.'

Bill Forward could see it was going to be a late night. He moved out of the way of the police photographer, who was taking various angles of the body. Turning to the pathologist, Bill asked, 'Anything you can tell me?'

'He was killed by a blow to the upper neck. Just below the skull. At the moment it looks as though the murder weapon was probably a log,' he said, pointing to a basket of logs beside the fire. 'There are some slivers of bark embedded in the deep grazing the blow caused. I'll be able to confirm that, and time of death, after the post mortem.'

Bill turned to the scenes of crime officer he'd met on a previous case. 'What can you tell me, Geoff?'

'Well, the room had been cleaned and the desk was well polished, so there's only *his* fingerprints here. Someone had put another log on the fire within the last couple of hours or so. But *he* could have done that, unless the killer did.'

Bill looked thoughtfully at the basket of logs before picking one up and feeling its weight. 'It's small enough to handle but heavy enough to give someone a fatal whack with. It wouldn't take long to burn either. And that would destroy fingerprints and any traces of blood.'

'Certainly would,' Marsh agreed.

'So our killer was either very lucky or bloody clever,' Bill said as he put the log back in the basket. 'Anything else, Geoff?'

'Only that the window behind the desk was open slightly. But it hasn't rained for a while and the ground is hard, so there are no footprints to suggest anyone entering from there. He could have opened the window himself to let the fumes from the fire out. I don't expect to find anything else here. So we shouldn't be long.'

Bill Forward took a look around the study, carefully looking in all the desk drawers. Then he checked the contents of Sir Reginald's trouser pockets, where he found a receipt from the MacCann hotel in Newcastle, along with his wallet and handkerchief. Putting everything in a plastic bag, he turned to Geoff Felix. 'Let the pathologist have the body when he wants it.' Bill beckoned Marsh to follow him as he left. Taking off his protective clothing in the hall he asked, 'Where can I go and interview?'

'There's a small television lounge,' said Marsh, pointing to a door across the hall. 'Who do you want first?'

'Let's have Doctor Wilson in.'

As Marsh went to the sitting room, Bill Forward went to the small lounge. In it was comfortable furniture facing a widescreen television set. As he turned an armchair to face the settee, the door opened and Marsh introduced David Wilson.

'Good evening, Doctor. I'm Detective Inspector Forward. Please sit down,' he said as he indicated the armchair.

Doctor Wilson sat and said, 'This is a terrible business, Inspector.'

'Yes, it is. I understand you examined Sir Reginald and pronounced him dead.'

The doctor nodded. 'The poor man must have died instantly. I checked his pulse but it was obvious he was dead. That's when I called the police.'

'I believe you and the other guests were playing a game at the time. A murder game, I think you said when you phoned.'

'Yes. That's why we were hiding in various rooms to avoid being a victim. There was an atmosphere of excitement and a lot of giggling from the ladies while they found a place to hide.'

'Do you remember whose idea it was to play that game?' Bill asked casually.

'Fiona's, I think. That's Lady Pace-Warren. Poor woman was in a state when she saw her husband. I've given her a sedative and she's resting in her bedroom. My wife is with her at the moment.'

'We'll want to speak to her ladyship as soon as we can, Doctor.'

'She'll be all right as long as you treat her gently, Inspector.'

'Yes, of course. I understand it was the housekeeper who found her employer?'

'Yes. It must have been an awful shock for her. I offered her a sedative but she refused. Mrs Romaine is made of sterner stuff than her mistress.'

'Where were you hiding?'

'In the bedroom, Inspector.'

'When you were hiding, did you notice anyone coming into the bedroom after you'd got there? Someone you recognized?'

'I couldn't see anyone as the curtains were drawn and all the lights were out. I could hear giggling but as to who they were I've no idea. I was too busy trying to hide. I ducked down beside the blanket chest at the foot of the bed.'

'Which bedroom was this?'

'The main guests' bedroom.'

'Thank you, Doctor. You'll need to stay in the house a little longer, in case I need you.'

'No problem. I shall go and see how my wife's getting on with Fiona. I'll let you know when she's well enough to interview.'

Sergeant Marsh saw the doctor out, then came back to join Bill Forward. Taking out his notebook he said, 'I made a note of what they all told me earlier. Just in case any of them deviate from what they tell *you*.'

'Good thinking, sunshine. We'll make a detective out of you yet. Let's have the housekeeper in.'

Mrs Romaine was shown into the room and sat in the armchair. She appeared much calmer than Bill expected. After introducing himself he said, 'It must have been quite a shock for you to find your employer like that.'

'It was totally unexpected. Awful.'

'Tell me. What made you go to the study?'

'I went to check the fire. Sir Reginald liked to keep it stoked up when he was working there in the evening. But when I saw him, I had to hurry out,' she said. 'I must have lost control and screamed. That's when her ladyship came across from the cloakroom.'

'So she was already down on this level?'

'Yes. I think she was hiding in the cloakroom with the young man Philippa Pane brought with her.'

Checking his notes, Marsh said, 'That would be Edward King?'

'Yes.'

To Marsh's surprise, his inspector changed the subject. 'The scenes of crime officer said a fresh log had been placed on the fire within the past two hours or so. Did you put the log on? Or would Sir Reginald have done that himself?'

She answered with slight hesitation. 'He didn't keep a dog and then do the barking himself, if you know what I mean.' Then she added thoughtfully, 'But as *I* didn't, I suppose he must have.'

'Just one other thing. When you went to find Doctor Wilson, where was he?'

'I called his name,' she replied, 'and he called back from the main guests' bedroom.'

'Well, thank you, Mrs Romaine.' The inspector smiled. 'Oh, by the way. Are the clothes her ladyship's wearing the same ones she had on when her husband came home?'

'Yes.'

'Thank you. You can join the others now.'

Marsh opened the door for her. As she left, Doctor Wilson arrived.

'You can go up and talk to Fiona now, Inspector. She's feeling a bit better.'

'Just a minute, Doctor.' Bill signalled Marsh to close the door. 'How well do you know Mrs Romaine?'

'Not very well. I only see her when I come here, which is not very often. Why do you ask?'

'It's just that you recognized her voice when she called for you. But you had your head down behind the blanket box hiding from the murderer,' Bill added with a friendly smile. 'In the game, I mean. Otherwise you could have become the victim.'

'I see what you mean. I hadn't thought of that.' He smiled. 'I recognized her voice because she called out with a sense of urgency. I'll show you to Fiona's bedroom, shall I?'

'I'd rather we saw her alone at the moment, Doctor,' said Bill. 'If you'll just tell us which room she's in, you can rejoin the other guests. We'll call you if we need you.'

David Wilson gave a shrug of acceptance. 'Top of the stairs and it's the first room on the right,' he informed them.

Dick Marsh saw the doctor out and closed the door after him. 'Why did you stop me asking Mrs Romaine what her ladyship was doing in the cloakroom with Edward King, sir?'

'Because, Sergeant, she wasn't in there with them and could only give you an "I don't know" or a wild guess as to whether they were groping each other behind the coats or not. I would rather hear it straight from the horse's mouth. Or in this case, both mouths. Let's go and ask her ladyship first.' Before they could get to the stairs, the doorbell rang. 'See who that is.'

Marsh opened the door. Two women constables had arrived. Bill Forward called two of the four PCs from the grounds into the house and asked one of each to wait in the hall while the remaining two waited outside the sitting room. 'I don't want anyone leaving until I give permission. Understood?' Turning to Marsh, he said, 'Come on. Let's go and see her ladyship.'

Fiona was sitting up and looking tired when they entered the bedroom. After introducing himself and Marsh, Bill Forward asked Sara Wilson to join the others in the sitting room. As she left, she gave a kindly smile to Fiona.

'Do you feel up to answering a few questions, ma'am?' Bill asked.

Her voice was quiet as she said, 'Yes, of course.'

'Can you think of anyone who would want to kill your husband?'

'Good heavens, no. He was a highly successful businessman. In business you make enemies, Inspector. But they don't kill you. They simply try to outsmart you.'

'The man you were in the cloakroom with. How well do you know *him*?'

Fiona was remembering his amorous advances to her. 'Come to think of it, I don't really know him at all. He was a boy that had a crush on me when we were young and we thought it would be fun to see him again.'

'When you say "we", who do you mean?' asked Sergeant Marsh.

'Philippa Pane. Apparently he's in town on his own and she asked if she could bring him tonight. Her regular gentleman friend couldn't be here.'

'So he's really *her* friend,' said Marsh.

Fiona seemed confused. 'I don't think she'd seen him for

years until they met this last day or so.' She looked as though she was trying to remember something.

Bill was curious. 'Is something bothering you, ma'am?'

'I've just remembered the phone call.'

'What phone call was that?' Bill asked.

'Well, it was a few days ago. I picked up the telephone in the sitting room to make a call but my husband was on the line. He was talking to someone who appeared to be threatening him. I should have hung up but my husband might have heard a click and he would have been furious if he thought I was listening in. So I just waited for the call to finish.'

'And what did you hear?' asked Marsh.

'It was a husky, almost whispering voice. It said, "stop it now, or you will pay the ultimate price."'

'That could have been referring to a property deal,' said Marsh.

'That's what I was thinking,' agreed Bill Forward.

Shaking her head, Fiona said, 'I don't think so. The voice was really sinister and threatening. I'd forgotten it until now.'

Dick Marsh asked, 'This voice. Was it male or female?'

'I think it was a man. But I can't be certain because it was very whispery. It was as though the caller didn't want to be heard by anyone at their end.'

Bill Forward listened with interest as Marsh continued. 'Was the call incoming or outgoing?'

She thought a moment. 'I can't be certain.'

'You said the call was in the past few days. Was it within two weeks or longer, would you say?' Marsh asked.

'Oh, I'm sure it was within two weeks.'

'Do you remember what time of day it was?'

'Afternoon, I think.'

'Not to worry. We can run a check on all the calls made and received during that period.'

Inspector Forward was pleased with his sergeant's efforts and said to him, 'If you've no more questions, Sergeant, would you get a female constable up here to sit with her ladyship. I'll see you in the interview room. With Edward King, please.'

Marsh nodded and left the room, leaving Fiona looking confused and obviously concerned by the phone call.

Bill Forward asked, 'Does the MacCann hotel in Newcastle mean anything to you?'

'No. Should it?'

'It isn't one your husband stays at when he's up that way?'

'He always stays at the Copthorne. Either there or the Holiday Inn. They're both four star.'

He waited for a PC to arrive before leaving Fiona in her care. 'You don't have to come down until you feel up to it, ma'am. If there's anything you want, please ask this police constable.'

'This was meant to be a really lovely, fun day.' She began to sob and the constable put a consoling arm around her.

CHAPTER SIX

It was established early in the interview that Edward King lived in Chelmsford, Essex, and had come to London two days earlier to look up some old friends from the past.

'Did these old friends include Fiona Pace-Warren?' the inspector asked.

'No. I didn't even know she was still in the area until Philippa told me,' King replied. 'Although I had often wondered about her. I used to fancy her when we were young and when I was told she'd got a title now, I was curious to see if it had changed her.'

'And had it?' Marsh asked.

King shook his head. 'She was always beautiful with a lovely nature. And still is.'

'Who told you about her title?'

'Philippa, when I met her yesterday.'

'So you had an address or phone number for Miss Pane. Had you kept in touch with her?'

'No. I went to the old address and found she still lived there. Bit of luck, that, because she knew all about Fiona and where she was now.'

'Is Philippa who you stayed with last night?' asked Marsh.

'Good heavens, no!' laughed King. 'I'm not that desperate. I stayed at a Travelodge. That's where I booked into when I arrived in London.'

'Are you married, Mr King?'

'No. Mind you, I came close to it once, but she became very possessive. And she was jealous if I so much as even smiled at another woman. It got ridiculous. And she was often away with her job.'

'What does she do?' Bill asked.

'She's an interior designer. I believe she's working at a hotel in Manchester at the moment. No doubt she's advising them to have the most expensive curtains. She was good at spending other people's money, especially mine.'

'And what do you do for a living, sir?' asked Marsh.

'I'm not doing anything at the moment. Until recently I was managing a travel agency. But it's been taken over and the new people had their own man to run it.'

'And so two days ago you decided to look up some people you hadn't seen for ages. What made you suddenly do that after all this time?' asked Bill.

King smiled. 'I was throwing out some old photographs and wondered what the old gang were doing these days. So, as I was at a loose end, I thought I'd come up to Chelsea and sniff around.'

'What were you doing in the cloakroom with her ladyship?'

'I was the detective in the game and Fiona had to show me where to wait. Unlike everyone else, I didn't know the layout of this house. I told your sergeant all this earlier.'

Marsh gave the inspector a confirming nod as he read from his notes. 'So you did, Mr King. Almost verbatim.'

'So there you were, alone with the beautiful woman you used to fancy. That must have been very pleasant for you, sir.' Bill smiled.

King grinned. 'I can think of better places than a cloak-room, Inspector.'

'I take it you never met her husband, sir,' said Marsh.

'I never laid eyes on him until I caught a glimpse of him in the study tonight, with those eyes just staring. Not a sight I shall forget in a hurry,' King said with a grimace.

'Do you know who the murderer was, sir?' Bill asked.

King looked bewildered. 'Do me a favour. I hardly knew who *anyone* was when I arrived here!'

'I meant in the murder game, sir.'

'Oh. I've no idea who had the jack of clubs, no.'

Bill Forward got up. 'Thank you, Mr King. Please rejoin the others. We shall try not to keep you too long.'

Marsh opened the door for King and as he closed it again, Bill said, 'What do you make of that one?'

'He had his answers off pat,' Marsh replied. 'But would he have told us he had a big crush on her ladyship if he'd been involved in her husband's death?'

'You could be right,' said Bill, with slight uncertainty. 'Let's have this Philippa Pane in.'

Before Marsh opened the door he said, 'I must warn you about this one, guv. She enjoys talking about everyone. A real mixer, I'd say.' He left the room.

Inspector Forward looked at his watch again and gave a deep sigh. He was wondering when he would get home and how Terry Kennedy was when Marsh ushered Philippa Pane into the room. Bill greeted her and offered her the armchair. Seeing her large frame, he realized why King was amused at the idea of him staying the night with her.

'How long have you lived at your current address, Miss Pane?'

'Since I was a child,' she said, adding with a broad grin, 'More years than I'm prepared to say, Inspector.'

Bill smiled. 'So Edward King had no trouble looking you up.'

'Oh no. And when I saw what a handsome hunk he'd turned into, I thought it would be nice for him to meet Fiona again. He always had the hots for her and I think she was delighted to see *him* again. If poor Reggie had not been killed, who knows what they might have got up to in that cloak-room? And good luck to her, I say.'

'You weren't a great admirer of Sir Reginald, were you?'

Philippa was only too pleased to answer. 'Any man with a young, beautiful wife who finds it necessary to have a bit on the side deserves all he gets.'

'Are you *certain* he had another woman somewhere? Or is it just gossip?' Bill asked.

'Everyone knew he was playing away from home.'

'So who do *you* think killed him?' asked Marsh.

'Probably a jealous husband who found out his wife was being bedded by an unpleasant property magnet. As to who that is, I've no idea. Mind you, I could be wrong,' she said thoughtfully. 'Otherwise it would mean that the jealous husband was one of the men here tonight, wouldn't it?'

'It would indeed,' said Bill.

'And that one of the girls here tonight has been letting Reggie get his end away.' She was enjoying the possibilities. 'Well now! There's a thought. I wonder who *that* could be?'

'Where were you hiding for the murder game, Miss Pane?' Marsh asked.

'In Fiona's bedroom, Sergeant.'

'Were you alone?' asked Bill.

'I touched a man's jacket as I groped my way to the wardrobe. He didn't say anything, so I don't know who it was. But my guess would be either Ken Morris or Paul Robson. It was too dark to be sure who *anyone* was. That's part of the fun, though. Being a mystery, I mean.'

45

'Yes. I suppose it is,' said Bill.

'And there's another mystery we were trying to solve just now,' Philippa said.

'And what was that?'

'Who had the jack of clubs and which one of us would they have killed if the game had carried on?'

Getting to his feet, Bill Forward said, 'If you find out the answer to either of those questions, perhaps you'll be kind enough to let me know.' He gave her his card and opened the door for her.

'I certainly will, Inspector. You can rely on that.'

'We'll try not to keep you much longer.' He smiled, closing the door after her. Then he said to Marsh, 'I see what you mean about her being a real mixer. She'd get anyone in trouble would that one. How many more have we got?'

'Three couples,' said Marsh, checking his notebook. 'They are just friends of her ladyship, as far as I can see. Two of the men are golfing buddies.'

'Right,' said Bill Forward. 'Let's have a married couple in for a change. With a bit of luck we might start making some headway with this case.'

'Right.'

As Marsh went to leave the room, Bill Forward remembered the one person he had almost forgotten. 'Before you get a couple, let's have the doctor's wife in.'

While he waited, he was going back in his mind over the interviews he had just had with Edward King, Philippa Pane and David Wilson. Suddenly the door opened and Geoff Felix looked in. 'The undertakers have collected the body and my team are finished,' he said.

'Thanks, Geoff.'

Geoff Felix left as Dick Marsh returned with Sara Wilson. Bill Forward spoke in a friendly manner. 'Well, Mrs Wilson.

It's been quite a night for you, hasn't it? First your husband is called and has to pronounce your host's death. Then you have to comfort his widow. Not the sort of evening you expected.'

'I still can't believe it happened. And just as we were about to play the murder game. It's quite bizarre,' said Sara.

'Where were you hiding for the game?'

'I was in the bathroom.'

'With your husband?'

'No. I don't know which room he went to.'

'Were you close friends with the Pace-Warrens?' Bill asked.

'My husband is their doctor but is seldom called on for any medical help. As for me, I like Fiona very much. She's such a lovely person.'

'I gather people were not as friendly towards her husband. By that, I mean he didn't seem too popular.'

Sara hesitated before she answered. 'He was a strange man. Not easy to get on with. He wasn't the welcoming type. I'm sure he didn't like Fiona inviting her friends round. He hardly ever came and joined us. Mind you, he always seemed to be away on business. To be brutally frank, I think he preferred making money to being with his lovely wife.'

'They didn't have any children?'

Sara shook her head. 'He didn't want any "snivelling brats" as he called them.'

'So why do you think he married her?'

'Because she is young and beautiful and other men envied him. It appealed to his masculine conceit. It's a strange relationship, Inspector. Not one that I can understand.'

Bill decided to take a chance and asked, 'Is it possible he might have had another woman somewhere?'

Sara became uncomfortable. 'Fiona's girlfriends, including myself, often wondered if Reggie had a bit on the side. But we had no proof. No proof at all. Just us spreading a bit of scandal, I suppose. I hope Fiona never finds out we said things like that about Reggie.'

'I must admit their relationship sounds unusual, to say the least. And what about his wife? How did she fulfil her natural desires while her husband was away?' Bill asked.

'I don't think Fiona had a liaison with *anyone*, if that's what you mean, Inspector. But if she did you could hardly blame her.'

'Then why did she marry Sir Reginald, do you think?'

'To be honest, I think she was a young woman who was flattered by the attentions of a titled man who could offer and provide everything a woman needs in the way of security. And he wanted a beautiful young woman at his side to satisfy his ego. I have to be fair and say he was more physically attractive when they first met – and less aggressive as well.'

Bill Forward nodded thoughtfully. 'So in a way, they were ideal for each other at the beginning.'

'Yes. In a strange sort of way, I suppose they were. But what Fiona will do now, God knows. At least her friends will keep an eye on her. She can be certain of that.'

'Well, thank you for your help. You and your husband are free to go whenever you wish.'

'Thank you, Inspector. At least she'll have Mrs Romaine with her tonight. My husband might give her something to help her sleep.'

As she got up, Dick Marsh opened the door for her and with a polite nod, she left.

'Interesting the way the women all disliked the victim but found his wife lovely,' said Marsh.

'Yes, isn't it. Who's next?'

'Andrew and Janet Davis. He's a self-employed ghost writer and works from home. She doesn't work.'

'Right. Wheel them in. I've never met anyone who writes for a ghost.'

The inspector went through the same questions as he had asked almost everyone else and it was Andrew who did most of the answering. He said he was hiding with his wife behind the bay-window curtains on the first-floor landing. It was when Bill mentioned the possibility of Sir Reginald having another woman somewhere that Janet began to chuckle.

'If you asked Philippa Pane that question, I'd love to know what *she* said.'

Andrew was obviously annoyed and said, 'There's no need to bring Philippa up, Janet. She's a troublemaker and would say anything to cause a stir.'

'All right. Sorry, Andrew. But you know what she said about Reggie when she phoned you.'

'And what was that, Mrs Davis?' Bill asked.

Andrew quickly answered for her. 'She wondered if I'd heard about Reggie and another woman, Inspector. Well, I hadn't and I warned her about spreading rumours like that. Like I told Janet, I had never heard that about Reggie and put it down to Philippa trying to cause trouble.'

Sensing Janet's discomfort, Bill asked her, 'Had *you* ever heard that about Sir Reginald, Mrs Davis?'

She and Andrew exchanged glances before she said, 'There had been gossip to that effect, yes. Just as there had been talk about all the men fancying Fiona and wanting to jump into bed with her.'

'Isn't that why women fuss over their make-up and clothes, to look attractive to the men?' Bill smiled. 'I know my wife does, and it works. I still find her very attractive. But getting back to tonight, is there anyone you can think of that would want to kill Sir Reginald? Or *have* him killed?'

'Good Lord, no,' said Andrew. 'And why the devil he was I can't imagine. Can you, Janet?'

She hesitated, and then said, 'A lot of people found him unpleasant, but I can't think of anyone who would resort to murdering him. And the thought of someone killing him while we were enjoying ourselves is horrible. Especially as nobody heard anything. It's something you read about happening but not to someone you know.'

Bill Forward nodded in agreement. 'I know you're a writer, Mr Davis. What are you working on now?'

Andrew laughed. 'I'm a ghost writer, Inspector. So I have to try and make other people's ideas and stories readable and clean up the mess they make of their own efforts. At the moment I'm looking at the history of poverty in Dickensian London. Not exactly thrilling but it pays our bills.'

'Well, good luck with it. I don't think there's anything else at the moment so you can go home now. And thank you for your time.'

'Thank you, Inspector. I do hope you catch the person who killed Reggie, for all our sakes. Otherwise we'll all be wondering which one of us actually slipped away to kill him,' said Andrew. 'If you should need us for anything else, you know where to find us.'

'I've got your address,' Marsh said as he saw them out.

'What did you make of those two, Sergeant?'

'Interesting the way he thought one of the party might have slipped away to kill their host. He's the only one to come up with that theory. Maybe it's because he's a writer.'

'It's an interesting thought, just the same,' said Bill. 'Who have we got next?'

'Ken and Angie Morris. He's an accountant.'

'Oh, a money juggler. Show them in.'

Marsh went to the sitting room and found it empty apart

from Mrs Romaine who was tidying up. 'Have you seen the Morrises?' he asked her.

'They're in the dining room with Mr and Mrs Robson, sir.'

Both couples were chatting as he entered the room. 'We'd like to see Mr and Mrs Morris, please,' said Marsh. 'We won't be long,' he told the Robsons.

'That's all right,' said Paul Robson, smiling. 'This food wants finishing up anyway. And I could do with a snack,' he added, patting his portly stomach.

Marsh introduced the Morrises to Bill Forward, who waited for them to be seated. 'I understand you're an accountant, Mr Morris,' said Bill.

'I am, yes.'

'Were you Sir Reginald's accountant?'

'Only for a brief time, Inspector. I found his methods of tax avoidance completely unacceptable. So we parted company and I kept my reputation for professional ethics in tact.'

'But you remained friends?'

'Angie and I remained friends with Fiona. We rarely saw her husband again. Neither of us liked the man to be honest.'

'It must have been difficult for *you*, Mrs Morris. You being friendly with his wife but not him.'

'Fiona knew that her friends didn't like the man, and we rarely came to the house when he was home. Normally we would only see each other when we went shopping or had a meal together. She seldom mentioned him except to say that he was away somewhere on business. But she never ran him down and we have to admire her loyalty there.'

'Yes, indeed,' Bill said. Then he asked, 'Where were you hiding for the game?'

'We were together in the single bedroom,' said Ken.

'Oh, is that where we were?' asked Angie. 'It was so dark I didn't know who I was with or where I was.'

'Were you surprised when you heard that Sir Reginald was killed in his study tonight?'

'Yes, of course we were. For someone to kill him when the house was full of people was a complete shock. It's so unreal,' Ken replied.

'I can't believe that none of us heard anything. It's really scary to know that somebody actually did it, then vanished,' said Angie.

'Maybe they didn't vanish. Perhaps they're still here, hiding in a cupboard,' joked Ken.

Angie shivered. 'Don't, Ken. Not even in fun.'

'You were all talking about it while you were together in the sitting room. Did anyone come up with an idea as to who might have done it, and why?' asked Marsh.

'Philippa Pane was convinced Reggie was having an affair and that it was a revenge killing by a jealous husband,' said Ken. 'The way he was always out crumpet-hunting, she could be right,' he added. 'Everyone guessed that he had a bit of spare somewhere.'

'We didn't know for certain, but it was always suspected that Reggie had got something other than business to keep him away,' Angie said.

'But no idea *who* this woman was?' asked Bill.

'No,' Ken said reluctantly. 'Nobody local though. Bound to be a woman up north, I imagine.'

'He was always going up north,' Angie added.

'Well, thank you both. I think we can leave it at that for now,' said Bill. 'We'll be in touch if we need you.'

After the Morrises had left, Bill Forward said, 'Bloody funny that nearly everyone thinks the victim had a woman on the side but no idea who she is or which town she comes from. Get a photo of Sir Reginald and ask the lads in Newcastle to confirm it was him in the MacCann hotel and who he was with. Ten to one he didn't use his own name. Anyway, we can do a bit of digging and see what we come up with.'

'I'll get on to it as soon as we've finished here. Our last couple are Paul and Sheila Robson. He's a financial advisor and she does his paperwork et cetera.'

'She'll be down on his tax return as his secretary,' said Bill.

'Probably,' said Marsh, smiling. 'Are you ready for them?'

'Yes. Let's get it over with.'

Paul Robson was finishing a sandwich as he was shown into the television lounge. An overweight man in his mid forties, he was a gregarious type and totally opposite to his wife, who was a quiet woman in her late thirties.

'Well, this is not exactly how we expected the party to finish,' said Paul. 'Fiona's parties normally go off with a bang, Inspector. Not with someone bashing in some poor bugger's brain. We couldn't believe it when Doc Wilson told us. Could we, Sheila?'

'I still can't,' his wife replied.

'Where were you hiding when the game started?' Bill asked.

'I hid in a wardrobe. Where were you, Sheila?'

'I was with a couple of people beside the bed in Fiona's room. I think one of them was the man with Philippa. Or it might have been someone else. It was so dark I can't be sure. And we didn't speak so as not to give ourselves away to the murderer.'

'So you've no idea who killed Sir Reginald?' Bill enquired.

'How would we know? We were hiding,' said Paul.

'But he could have been killed before you started playing any games.'

'I hadn't thought of that,' said Paul.

'Were you the financial advisor to Sir Reginald, sir?'

'Perish the thought.' Paul scowled, and added, 'I gave him a friendly tip on some shares once. He made a fortune and didn't even offer me an orange at Christmas! No, Inspector. My clients are a lot nicer than that bugger.'

'So you have no idea what he did with his money.'

'Ken and I always said he raped and robbed. He liked the women, did Reggie. And he was ruthless when it came to money.'

'Well, I don't think there's anything more at the moment. Thank you both for waiting. We'll be in touch if there's anything else we need you for.'

Paul got to the door and said, 'Is it all right if I grab a sandwich from the dining room? It seems a shame to waste all the food that's left in there.'

Sheila gave him a reprimanding look. 'Don't be a pig. You're fat enough already. Come on.'

After the Morrises had gone, Bill looked at his watch. 'It's almost ten thirty and I think we can call it a day. I'm dying for a cup of coffee.'

'Shall I ask the housekeeper for some?' Marsh asked.

'Don't bother, sunshine. I'll get one at home. And Marsh.'

'Yes, sir?'

'You get home too. Leave Newcastle till the morning. You've had a long day, so get your beauty sleep. We've got things to do tomorrow.'

'I'll get a photograph of Sir Reginald from the housekeeper before I leave. I want to get it up to the Newcastle lads first thing,' said Marsh.

'Your enthusiasm does you credit, Sergeant. Before you know it, you'll be chief constable. Good night.'

'Good night, sir.' Marsh was beginning to get used to his inspector's sense of humour and enjoyed his praise, even if it was said tongue in cheek. He was remembering what Dave

Norris had said about Bill Forward: 'He's a bloody good copper. You can learn a lot from him.' But Marsh wondered what his inspector was *really* thinking about the people they had been interviewing this evening. There was something about Inspector Forward that told him he was a copper who wouldn't share his thoughts until he was good and ready to do so. A bloody good copper he might be, but he could be frustrating to work with at times. With that going through his mind, Marsh got the photograph from Mrs Romaine and left the house.

CHAPTER SEVEN

Sergeant Marsh was already at his desk when Bill Forward arrived at 8.45. Being Sunday it was quieter than usual and they hoped to make some progress with their investigation.

'Morning, sir. Sleep well?'

'Not really. The brain kept going over and over last night's carry-on. Then I had a phone message from Father O'Connor to say that Terry Kennedy was starting to come out of the coma and he'll be at the hospital as soon as he finishes the morning service. I'm off there as soon as I pick up the photograph of Tony Farrow. Have you been on to Newcastle yet?' Bill asked as he took Farrow's photograph from his drawer.

'Yes, I have. I sent the photo to them about half an hour ago. Now we shall have to wait and see if the MacCann hotel recognizes Sir Reginald. The photograph was an old one the housekeeper found at the back of his desk drawer. It was one of him smiling, by the way. As he was with a lady friend at the hotel, he probably *was* smiling.' Marsh grinned.

'I wish I could be as bright as you at this time in the morning. Right, I'm off. Fingers crossed that young Terry's going to be OK. And that he recognizes our friend Farrow. Won't be long.' Bill Forward hurried out to his car.

As he left, Dick Marsh typed out a list of people they had interviewed at Stafford House yesterday evening.

When Bill Forward arrived at the hospital, he went straight to Terry Kennedy's room. Terry gave a weak smile as he saw his visitor.

'Hello, Mr Forward.'

'Hello, lad.' Bill smiled. 'How are you feeling?'

'Not too good at the moment. A bit bruised.'

Bill gave the boy's hand a pat. 'Just one question, lad. Then I'll leave you in peace.' He took the photograph from his pocket and showed it to Terry. 'Is this the man that beat you up?'

Terry looked at the photograph and shook his head. 'I've never seen him before. Who is he?'

Bill was unable to hide his disappointment. 'You're quite sure?'

'Positive,' Terry insisted, his voice sounding tired. 'The bloke that set about me was young, and on drugs, I reckon. He was after money. When I told him I hadn't got any he went potty. Who's this bloke?'

'Someone who uses his fists instead of his brains,' said Bill, putting the photograph in his pocket. 'I'm glad to see you looking more like your old self again. You rest now. I'll come and see you again soon.'

'Goodbye,' said Terry. 'Thanks for coming.'

Back in the office, Bill gave Marsh the news that Farrow was not Terry's attacker.

'Never mind, it was worth a try,' said Marsh.

Bill sat at his desk and put the photograph of Farrow back in the drawer. 'I was hoping it was him. Then I could have closed the file on this. But I'd still like to know why he was with Mandy Lucas the other night.'

Marsh was confused. 'Who exactly *is* Mandy Lucas?'

'She was on the game at the age of sixteen. Then she packed it in after a year. She always said that she did it because her mother hadn't got the money to pay for food and heating. Her father had buggered off so there was no money coming in. He disappeared and went to Spain with his new lady. Mandy always insisted that her days on the streets were for the reason she gave. And, as far as I know, she never turned to prostitution again. But with Farrow's record, I'd like to know what she was doing with him. Call it professional curiosity but I think I'll have a word with Mandy. Any chance of a coffee?'

At that moment a PC came in with some papers for Marsh.

'Perfect timing, Constable,' said Bill. 'Could you get me some coffee? I'm in desperate need of caffeine.'

The constable was used to the constant demand for coffee from that office. 'Right away, sir,' she said.

'What are those papers she brought in?' asked Bill.

'I made out a list of the people we interviewed last night and she ran me off some copies. I thought we might want to go over them later. You know, refresh our memories on what they said and what impression they made on us.'

'I wonder if I was as efficient as you when I was your age,' said Bill. 'I suppose I must have been or I wouldn't be your senior officer, would I?' He smiled.

Marsh wasn't sure whether it was a compliment or a put-down and changed the subject. 'Have you got an address for Mandy Lucas?' he asked.

'Don't get too anxious to see her. Like I said, I don't think she's on the game these days.'

'I thought it was *you* that wanted to see her, sir,' Marsh retorted with a grin.

'What I said was, have a *word* with her. And now you can

look up her number for me. It's under Lucas and it's in Melton Street. Her mother will answer if Mandy's not there.'

While Marsh was looking up the number, a woman from the canteen arrived with two mugs of coffee and some sugar on a tray. 'Here's your coffees. One black, one white but I couldn't remember if you both took sugar, so it's on the tray.' She put the tray on Bill's desk and left.

'Thank you, Barbara,' Bill called after her and started drinking.

Marsh found the number and dialled. A woman answered.

'Hello, yes?'

'Mrs Lucas?'

'Speaking.'

'I have DI Forward for you.'

Bill put the mug down and picked up his extension. 'Hello, Mrs Lucas. Is your Mandy about?'

'She's just got out of the bath, Mr Forward. Not in any trouble, is she?'

'No, Mrs Lucas. I'm hoping she can put me in touch with someone, that's all. Can I have a word, please?'

'Hang on. I'll give her a call.'

After a moment he heard Mandy's voice. 'Hello, Mr Forward. What can I do for you?'

'Hello, Mandy. I'll keep this brief. Were you with Tony Farrow last night?'

'No,' she said. 'He left here yesterday morning for Cardiff. Is he all right?'

'Yes, as far as I know. When did you last speak to him?'

'Yesterday evening.'

'What time?'

'It was about eight thirty when he telephoned me.'

'Where was that from?'

'His cousin's place in Cardiff.'

'Have you got the Cardiff number? It's important, Mandy.'

'I've got it in my purse. Hold on a minute. Here it is. Are you sure he's all right?' She sounded anxious as she gave him the number.

'Don't worry. I just wanted to know where he was in case I need to speak to him. He might be able to help me with something, that's all. Thanks for the number.'

'That's OK.'

He hung up. 'It looks as though Farrow was miles away in Cardiff when Sir Reginald was killed. In which case, we're back to square one again. Let's have a look at that list you made. There might be something we were too tired to notice last night.' He began dialling a number as Marsh took a copy of the list to him.

'Who are you calling, sir?'

'Tony Farrow's cousin. Before Mandy has a chance to tell Farrow I was asking about him. Just a precaution.'

'Don't you trust her then?'

'I'm a policeman, Marsh. I was trained not to trust anybody.' When a man answered the Cardiff number, Bill spoke in a friendly manner. 'Hello, sir. Is Tony Farrow there?'

'Who's calling?'

'My name is Forward. Mr Farrow and I have a mutual friend.'

'I'm Tony Farrow. Who's this mutual friend?'

'Mandy Lucas.'

'Is she all right? Nothing's happened to her, has it?'

'She's fine. I just finished talking to her.'

'So what is it you want?'

'I want to know where you were yesterday evening. I have to tell you that I'm a detective inspector at Chelsea and think you might be able to assist us with our enquiries, sir.'

Bill could tell the man sounded uneasy as he asked, 'What is it you want to know?'

'Where you were yesterday evening?' Bill repeated.

'Oh, yes. Well, I left London coach station just after lunch and arrived here at my cousin's just before seven.'

'And when will you be returning, sir?'

'I don't know. Maybe next week, I haven't decided.'

'Got an open return ticket, then.'

'No. My cousin might drive into London or I might come on the train. It all depends. Look, why are you asking me all this? Am I supposed to have done something?'

'Someone answering your description was seen in Chelsea yesterday evening. And we are checking on the movements of anyone who fits that description. And as you were seen in the area on Friday evening with Mandy Lucas, I'm simply trying to establish whether you were in Chelsea yesterday evening.'

'Well, I wasn't,' he said angrily, 'so go and look somewhere else. I've told you I was here in Cardiff. Mandy knows I was here because I phoned her last night, to let her know I'd arrived. She must have told you that.'

'Well, sorry to have bothered you. But we have our job to do, you understand.'

'Yes, I know. But if you've finished, I'd like to get on.'

'Thank you for your help, Mr Farrow. I shan't bother you again, unless of course I have to. Goodbye, sir.' Bill hung up and turned to Marsh. 'Not a happy man, I'd say. I don't think we can eliminate him just yet. I'd like you to check Mandy's phone calls last night and see if there *was* one from this Cardiff number.' As he passed the number to Marsh, his telephone rang and he answered it. 'DI Forward.'

'It's Superintendent Lamb. Just wondering if you're getting anywhere with the Pace-Warren murder?'

'It's early days yet, sir.'

'Well, let me know if you need any help. I'd like this one wrapped up as soon as possible. Important man was Sir Reginald and the press will be on it like vultures.'

'I'll be going round to the house this morning. I've got one or two things to sort out and I want to look at the study again.'

'Have you got a suspect yet?' asked Lamb.

'Yes. Twelve of them!'

'Well, like I said. Just ask if you need someone to join your team.'

'I will, sir.'

'Good luck, Forward.'

'Thank you, sir. Something tells me I'm going to *need* luck with this one.' He hung up.

Despite it being early on Sunday morning, Philippa Pane was soon on the phone to Sara Wilson.

'Hello, Sara. What a night *that* was! It wasn't till I got home that it dawned on me poor Fiona was left all alone to face the reality of poor Reggie's murder. Awful for her to be in the bed without him next to her.'

Sara tried to hide her impatience. 'It's been a bad night for all of us who were there. I hardly slept at all and was hoping to catch up on some sleep when the phone rang just now.'

'Sorry if I've disturbed you, Sara. I thought you might want someone to talk to about last night, that's all. But I forgot that you've got David. What a good thing he was there to look after Fiona before all those forensic people arrived. You must be very proud of him. I know I would be if he was *my* husband.'

'Thank you for the call. And now, if you'll excuse me.'

'Before you go. What did you think of my escort? Rather dishy, isn't he?'

Sara wanted desperately to hang up but couldn't resist saying, 'I thought it was Fiona that he was interested in.'

'Oh, it *was*. That's why I brought him. And that's why Fiona got into the cloakroom with him. If poor Reggie hadn't been killed the mind boggles as to what they might have got up to.'

Sara became curious. 'So they'd known each other before, had they?'

'Oh yes, years ago. But I mustn't tell tales out of school. Give my regards to David. Tell him I'm sorry if I've disturbed him.'

'He isn't here. He went to visit Fiona to see how she is this morning.'

'He must be the envy of most men. After all, he would see more of her body than they could. Being a doctor, I mean.'

Angry at Philippa's remark, Sara hung up.

Sergeant Marsh received the call he was waiting for and looked pleased as he hung up. 'That was Newcastle,' he told Bill. 'They didn't waste any time in getting what we want to know.'

'So tell me.'

'They showed the photograph of Sir Reginald to the receptionist that was on duty on Friday. He checked in as Mr R. Carrington with his attractive brunette *wife*.'

'Did he now? Well, well. Had he been there before, did she say?'

'They asked her that but she didn't remember seeing him before.'

'I think it's time to pay another visit to Stafford House. Come on, Sergeant.'

Bill Forward was on his way to Stafford House with Sergeant Marsh just before 10 a.m. He thought it was a reasonable hour to continue his investigation and hoped Lady Pace-Warren was feeling up to answering any questions.

'Fancy the super offering you an extra man on this case. Was he friendly with Sir Reginald, sir?' asked Marsh.

'Don't think so. But if he can get a quick result, it would be a leg-up towards his promotion to chief super, wouldn't it? And that's what he'll be looking for.'

'Yes. While we do all the work he gets the glory, you mean.'

Bill nodded and said, 'Before we interview Lady Pace-Warren, there's something I want to try.'

'What's that?'

'Well, the ground was hard last night and the forensic boys couldn't see any sign of footprints outside the study window. I want to see if I can thump you on the back of the neck with a log from outside the window, and then toss the log onto the fire. That's what I want to do, sunshine. And I want to do it before we get any rain to soften the ground up.'

'I wouldn't have thought anyone could do that from *outside*. Not while Sir Reginald was sitting down. And we know he was sitting down because of the position his body was in when he was found.'

'That's true. But with nothing much to go on at the moment, I want to give it a try. And if it's not possible, we'll be certain the murder was committed by someone who was *inside* the study.'

As they turned into Chart Gardens, they saw Doctor Wilson's car leaving Stafford House. He was looking preoccupied and drove past without acknowledging them.

Mrs Romaine opened the front door and took them to the sitting room, where Fiona was sitting. She looked surprised.

'Oh, it's you, Inspector. I thought it was David Wilson coming back for something.'

'No, I'm afraid it's us again, ma'am,' he said. 'We're sorry to trouble you, but there are some things we'd like to discuss, regarding last night. If you feel up to answering some questions, that is.'

'Yes, of course. Please sit down, gentlemen.'

'Before we do, we'd like to have another look at the study.'

She suddenly became uncomfortable. 'I do hope you don't want me there with you. I don't think I'm quite ready to go into that room just yet.'

'You can stay here,' Bill said kindly. 'We shan't be long.'

The sergeant followed him from the room. 'For a lady that's been through a traumatic experience, she still looks bloody gorgeous,' Marsh said quietly.

'She certainly does,' agreed Bill.

They arrived at the study and Marsh sat at the desk and opened the window. As he waited for Bill to get outside, his mobile rang.

'Yes? That's right. And that was definitely yesterday? Thank you. Goodbye.' He turned to Bill, who had just come to the window. 'That was the phone company. Mandy was telling the truth. She received a call from the Cardiff number at 7.38 p.m. last night. So Farrow *was* in Cardiff as he said.'

Inspector Forward frowned in disappointment. 'Bugger. Never mind. Let's get on with our experiment.' He took a log from the stack near the window and, holding it firmly in one hand, reached through the window, trying to reach the back of Marsh's head. 'Even with a longer arm I couldn't hit you. And if you stood up you'd still be out of reach. Shut the window and we'll go back and see her ladyship.'

As they walked into the hall, Mrs Romaine came from the sitting room.

'I've just taken her ladyship some coffee. Would you gentlemen like some?' she asked.

'That's very kind, thank you,' said Bill, and he and Marsh went into the sitting room.

'Please sit down,' said Fiona.

Bill and Marsh sat on the settee and Bill explained, 'We've just carried out an experiment that suggests your husband was killed by someone from inside the house.'

Fiona was shocked. 'But the only people here, apart from Mrs Romaine and myself, were my friends. Are you telling me that one of *them* killed Reggie?'

'Yes, unless it was someone who called at the house earlier and hid inside or came back later and let themselves in. There was no sign of a forced entry anywhere or anyone breaking in.'

'Did you have any visitors earlier in the day?' Marsh asked.

The housekeeper returned with two coffees and put the tray on a small table.

'Mrs Romaine, did we have any visitors yesterday? Before the dinner party, I mean,' Fiona asked her.

'There was only the butcher and the man to read the meters.'

'Did either of them come into the house?' asked Bill.

'Well, the butcher came into the kitchen. He always does when he delivers here. And the man had to come into the cloakroom to read the electric meter. The gas one is in its own box outside,' she explained.

'Were you with the meter man all the time?'

'No. But he was only here for a few minutes.'

'And did he arrive at the front or back door?'

'The front, but I asked him to go to the back door. I don't like the tradesmen walking through the hall after I've cleaned it.'

'Was he the regular man?' asked Marsh.

'No. He had to ask where the meter was, so he must have been new.'

'Which company was he from?' Bill asked her.

'It's Power-On. We've only just switched over to them.'

'Would you recognize the man if you saw him again?'

She thought for a moment. 'Yes. I think so.'

'Well, thank you, Mrs Romaine. And thanks again for the coffee.' Bill smiled as he watched her leave. 'It must be nice to have your housekeeper living with you at a time like this, ma'am,' he told Fiona.

'It was very kind of her to stay last night. I didn't want to be on my own after my guests left. But she doesn't live here Inspector. She has her own apartment in the mews round the corner.'

'Oh, I see. I thought that being a housekeeper she lived on the premises.'

'Strictly speaking, she isn't a housekeeper. She came to me as a daily woman after her husband died three years ago. For just two days a week at first. But now she comes whenever we have a dinner party or people in for tea, and comes most days to tidy up and make the beds. She prefers housekeeper rather than daily woman, so that's how she's known.'

'I see. Now, when I searched the desk last night, I could find no records of your husband's business dealings. And they didn't appear to be anywhere in the study. Do you know where he kept them?'

She looked puzzled. 'I'm sorry, but unless they're in his desk or filing cabinet, I'm afraid I don't.'

'You told me you had never heard of the MacCann hotel in Newcastle and that you didn't think your husband had stayed there.'

'That's right.'

'Well, I'm afraid I have to tell you that he *did* stay there on Friday night. And he was with a lady. An attractive brunette that he said was his wife, apparently.'

Fiona became deflated but not shocked. 'So the rumours about him having a woman somewhere were true.' She sighed. 'And *she* must have been the meeting he said he had to attend on Friday evening. Do you know who the woman was?'

'Not at the moment.'

'Oh God, I hope Philippa Pane never finds out about this. The whole world will know if she does and I'll be humiliated.'

Bill didn't enjoy this part of his job. 'Does the name Carrington mean anything to you?'

Fiona shook her head. 'Should it?'

'It was the name he used at the hotel. I just wondered if it had any significance, that's all.' Bill could see she was holding back a tear and got up, signalling Marsh to follow him. 'We'll leave you now, ma'am. If there's anything else we'll be in touch.'

He and Marsh left and went towards the kitchen, where Mrs Romaine was preparing vegetables for Sunday lunch. 'I think her ladyship needs some company. We'll see ourselves out.' Mrs Romaine gave an understanding nod, removed her apron, and went to the sitting room.

As soon as she had gone, Bill went to the back kitchen door and opened it. He saw that it had an old Victorian lock with a large key, which was the only way to secure the door, as a sliding bolt was broken. He closed the door and turned the key, trying the door for any movement.

'Well, this feels secure enough but I wouldn't think it would pass an insurance scrutiny,' he said.

'And have you noticed the house isn't alarmed?' said Marsh. 'Strange, that.'

'Yes, it is. Considering Sir Reginald appeared to be such a fusspot. Come on. We'll go out the back way. And when I get to the office, remind me to call Power-On and check if they had a man here yesterday.'

'Won't they be closed on a Sunday apart from emergencies?'

'This *is* an emergency. Come on.'

Mandy Lucas was hoping for a phone call and when it came she was relieved to hear Tony Farrow's voice.

'Hello, love. How are you?' he asked.

'A bit worried. Where are you now?'

'According to the police I'm somewhere in Wales,' he laughed. 'You must have been convincing when that copper called you, because he phoned my cousin as soon as he finished talking to you. He really believed he was talking to me and that I was in Cardiff. So now we don't have to worry any more. I'll see you in a few days when all this has blown over.'

'But where are you?'

'What you don't know you can't tell, so just relax and trust me. All right, love?'

'Take care of yourself, won't you?'

'You know me. Don't worry. See you soon. Bye, love.'

Mandy put down the receiver but wished she felt as confident as Tony appeared to be.

Sergeant Marsh had received a fax from the telephone company with a list of calls made to and from Stafford House over the past three weeks. He was about to mention them when Bill Forward dialled the number for Power-On.

'This is Detective Inspector Forward, Chelsea CID. I'm investigating a murder and need to know if one of your men went to read a meter yesterday. The address is Stafford House, Chart Gardens, Chelsea. Yes, I'll hold.' After a few moments, he was given the reply. 'You're absolutely positive that nobody went there from Power-On? I see … Yes. Thanks for your help.' He replaced the receiver. 'Well, it seems the man who went there yesterday *was* an impostor. What have you got there?'

'A list of incoming and outgoing phone calls at Stafford House. Some of them I recognize as those of the guests there last night. As for the others, we'll have to check them with her ladyship and see if she knows any of them.'

'You can do that tomorrow. I'm more interested in the meter reader at the moment and whether he's the killer or not.'

'Well, if he is, he'd have no trouble getting in, I imagine. He could have slipped the key out for a minute while the house-keeper wasn't looking. Taken a quick impression, probably while he was in the cloakroom pretending to read the meter, then slipped it back again on his way out.'

Bill nodded in agreement. 'Well, unless she left the kitchen door unlocked, your assumption is more than likely. But he'd have to get the old key out in order to put the new one in. And unless he was lucky, that would make a noise as it fell to the floor.' He became thoughtful and said, 'Unless he put some-thing into the lock to stop it closing. Then, even if she tried in vain to turn the key, she wouldn't have bothered anyone about that during the party. Not while she was concerned with their food and drinks. But who *was* our meter man?'

'It could have been the one that her ladyship thought was threatening her husband on the phone. She might have been right about that call all along. I'll tick the calls on this list that are local and see if I can check the others tomorrow.'

'Good idea. Let's go and get a pre-lunch drink. I think we both need one. What are you doing about lunch?'

'I don't know. I haven't planned anything.'

'Surely you've got a girlfriend you'd like to be with who could do you a Sunday roast?'

Marsh smiled. 'You're a good policeman, sir, but I know when you're searching for information.'

'So? Answer the question.'

'I did have a girlfriend but the job came between us. You know what it's like. Even before I joined CID, I would get called out at various times of the night. Uniform have a tough time as well. Much as we regretted it, we cancelled our future plans and went our separate ways.'

'Do you keep in touch?'

'No. She found someone else and went to live in Devon.'

'Never mind, sunshine,' said Bill, with a quiet under-standing. 'You'll find someone else when you least expect it. I know, because I did. How she puts up with me I'll never know. But she does. I'm a lucky man.'

Marsh was surprised at his inspector's sincerity. 'I'd like to meet her one day,' he said.

Bill picked up the phone and dialled. 'Hello, love. What have you got planned for lunch?'

'I thought we'd have a roast tonight,' said Jane.

'That's tonight. What about lunch. Do you fancy something at the Italian? They're open. I'm taking Marsh there and he'd like to meet you. You can be ready in ten minutes, can't you?'

'Well, yes, if you're serious.'

'Right. We'll pick you up. Oh, you've got the number there, so give them a ring and book it, will you?'

'OK,' said Jane.

'And if they're full try the other one you like. See you soon, love. Bye.' He looked at Marsh. 'You like Italian, don't you?'

'Yes. Yes, I do,' Marsh said, taken completely by surprise.

'Good. We'll have a nice bottle of red with the meal. It was recommended by Father O'Connor. And he certainly knows his wines.' He got up from his desk and put his coat on. 'Right, come on, let's go, shall we?'

Marsh walked with Bill Forward to the car park, wondering what had brought on this friendly mood from his superior.

CHAPTER EIGHT

Angie Morris had paid what she considered a dutiful visit and was about to leave. 'Thank you for coming, Angie. It was very thoughtful of you.' As Fiona opened the front door for her, she was surprised to see Edward standing there. 'Edward! You gave me quite a shock.'

'Sorry,' he said. 'You gave me a shock too. I was just about to ring the bell as you opened the door.'

Angie was intrigued by his presence and sorry to be leaving.

'I'm Angie. We met last night.'

'Yes. I remember,' he said.

Fiona was surprised at his being there but wanted to get rid of Angie before finding out why he'd come.

'Angie is an old friend and was just leaving after very kindly paying me a visit,' Fiona explained. 'Please don't stand there in the cold, Edward. Go into the sitting room. I'll be with you as soon as I've seen Angie off.'

Edward smiled at Angie and went into the house.

'Lucky you,' said Angie to Fiona.

'What do you mean?'

'Well, at least he came alone instead of bringing the dreaded Philippa with him,' said Angie. 'According to the scandal queen, he used to fancy you like mad. So I'm sure you can do without *her* turning up. I'll be off now, Fiona. Take care of yourself.'

'I will. Goodbye, Angie.' She closed the door with a sigh of relief and went to the sitting room.

Edward was standing with his back to the fire and looked at her with concern. 'I hope you don't mind me coming but I had to see you. How are you bearing up?'

'Not too bad really,' she said.

He sat on the settee and patted the space next to him, inviting her to sit there. After a moment's hesitation she went and sat next to him. Edward took her hand and held it.

'When I was invited to come here last night I wondered what you would be like after all these years and couldn't believe my eyes when I saw you,' he said.

'Had I changed *that* much?' she asked.

'You were far more beautiful than I could have imagined,' he said, giving her hand an affectionate squeeze.

She liked the way he said it and smiled. 'I was also surprised to see that the skinny teenager I knew had become such a handsome man.' She gently slid her hand free from his and said, 'I remember your father coming to the school to take you out sometimes. And he was a good-looking man. You must take after him. Are your parents still alive?'

'My mother died six years ago from a heart attack. And my father married a Canadian woman two years ago and now lives in Port Hope, Ontario. She's very nice and it pleases me to know he's happy again. We still keep in touch. What about your folks?'

'There's only my brother and myself. My parents were both killed in a road accident when I was twenty-two. They didn't like the idea of my marrying Reggie because of the age gap. And I don't think my father ever got to like my husband.

Even though he did have a title and took care of me, especially in the early days of our marriage. But then Reggie became very, very possessive and unpleasant to my friends, both male and female.'

'What about your brother?'

'He thought my marrying Reggie was disgusting and hasn't really kept in touch. He lives in Scotland with a wife I've never met. I get a card from them at Christmas and that's about all.'

'Is he older than you?'

'Yes. By two years.' Fiona laughed as she said, 'Well, we may not have met for a few years but we're certainly making up for lost time.'

Edward smiled and asked, 'Where's your housekeeper right now?'

'She's gone to her apartment for a while so that she can bath and change into some fresh clothes. She very kindly stayed here last night. In case I didn't sleep and needed company.'

'I thought she lived here with you.'

Fiona smiled. 'No. She got the meat in the oven before she went, so she'll be back later and get lunch for me. I would invite you to join me but no doubt you have other plans.'

'No. I've nothing planned. I'd love to stay. As long as you're sure it won't put you in a compromising position.'

'Mrs Romaine would be the soul of discretion. If you're worried that your wife might get to hear something, I think you are quite safe.' She smiled. 'As long as Philippa doesn't hear we had lunch together. Otherwise the whole of Chelsea would know.'

He gave her hand another squeeze and said, 'I certainly shan't tell my wife. I couldn't if I wanted to.'

She gave him a quizzical look and asked, 'Why?'

With a broad smile he said, 'Because I haven't got one.'

Fiona was curious why such a good-looking man had not been snapped up by someone and Edward explained about his ex-girlfriend and the trouble he'd had with her.

Fiona looked into his eyes and was convinced he was telling her the truth. 'I'm sorry you had that problem, Edward. I know exactly how you must feel. It seems we have both had bad luck with our partners. I learnt today that my husband stayed in a hotel on Friday night under an assumed name and with a woman he said was his wife.'

He put a comforting arm around her and held her close, Fiona didn't resist and felt remarkably at ease with him. Suddenly they heard Mrs Romaine call out, 'I'm back.'

Fiona quickly got up and opened the door, then called in reply, 'We're in the sitting room. I have a visitor who will be staying to have lunch with me.' She left the door partly open and moved to an armchair, where she sat and gave Edward a smile. Mrs Romaine came to the door and looked in. Politely, she acknowledged Edward without showing any surprise at him being there.

'There's enough for two,' she said. 'I'll set everything in the dining room and you can help yourselves. It's almost ready.'

'That will be fine. Thank you,' said Fiona.

'Would you like me to come and clear up when I get back from my sister's?' asked Mrs Romaine. 'It will be about six.'

Fiona shook her head. 'Don't worry about that. I can clear up after lunch. I might go and visit my friends after that. You have a nice time with your sister and I'll see you tomorrow.'

'Thank you, m'lady.' Mrs Romaine left the room, closing the door quietly behind her.

Edward waited until he could hear her footsteps crossing the hall to the kitchen before speaking. 'I seem to remember that it was she who interrupted us in the cloakroom last night,' he said with a quiet laugh.

'I hate to think what would have happened if Reggie had seen us in that cloakroom,' said Fiona. 'Being such a jealous man, he could be quite violent. Now here I am, alone with a man I haven't seen since we were teenagers, and I have no conscience at all.'

'I know what you mean. Strange, isn't it?' he said

Fiona smiled as she said, 'What I find strange is that I feel quite comfortable with you. Come on. Let's get some lunch.'

Edward followed her to the dining room, wondering where today would be leading them.

CHAPTER NINE

Angie Morris had arranged to meet Sheila Robson at the golf club. A table had been booked for a late lunch with their husbands, who would join them after their round of golf. Sheila was already in the bar when Angie arrived and, after greeting each other with an air-kiss on the cheek, she couldn't wait to tell her the news.

'Guess who arrived at Fiona's just as I was leaving?'

'Who?'

'The good-looking devil that turned up with Philippa last night. But this time he was on his own.'

'On his own? That's interesting.'

'Yes, how about that? He's the one that had a crush on her when they were in their teens, but hadn't met again until the party last night, according to Philippa. He looked surprised when he saw *me* there this morning. Do you think there might be something going on that we don't know about?'

'Well, we all guessed Reggie had a woman tucked away and wondered if Fiona put up with it simply because of the money and his title. But Sara Wilson wondered if Fiona was playing him at his own game and had a man of her own tucked away somewhere. Perhaps she had.' Sheila chuckled. 'Good luck to her if she did.'

'And that man conveniently escorted Philippa last night to remove all suspicion of what was going on behind Reggie's back, you mean? I can't believe that. Philippa would have known if that were true and told the world. And Fiona wouldn't have taken a chance like that. It's too risky. Reggie would have killed her,' said Angie.

'Perhaps that's why someone killed Reggie,' said Sheila.

'It makes you think, doesn't it?' said Angie.

'And wasn't he alone with Fiona while we were all hiding for the murder game? Hiding downstairs in the cloakroom, weren't they?' said Sheila.

Angie was deep in thought and said, 'The police think Reggie was killed by someone at the party. And the only one none of us had met before was this Edward. And now, with Reggie dead, he turns up, alone, to see Fiona this morning. Interesting, isn't it?'

'It certainly is,' said Sheila. 'We must see what the boys think when they come in. I don't know about you, but I could do with a drink.'

'Good idea. Thinking makes me thirsty.'

They ordered two gin and tonics and sat enjoying the drinks and the possibility of Fiona having a secret affair with Edward King.

The Italian lunch had been a satisfying one and Sergeant Marsh had got on well with Jane Forward.

'Let me share that with you, sir,' said Marsh as the bill arrived and Bill Forward took it off the plate.

'No, Marsh. In a moment of madness I invited *you*, remember?

'Well, thank you, sir. But next time it's on me.'

'I'll keep you to that.' Bill put the cash on the plate and got up. 'Better get back to work, I suppose. We've got a murderer to catch. Are you ready, love?' he asked Jane.

'Yes. That was a lovely surprise lunch. And it was nice to meet you at last, Sergeant.' She smiled.

'It was nice to meet you too,' said Marsh.

'I'll drop you back home, love, then Marsh and I can get back to the nick and see if that wine has clouded our judgement.'

When they got back to their office, Bill wanted to look through the interviews that Marsh had meticulously made a record of from last night. As Marsh lifted the file from his drawer he said, 'That was a lovely restaurant. It had a nice atmosphere.'

'That's where I saw Mandy Lucas and Farrow on our first visit,' Bill said. 'I still have a gut feeling that he's up to no good.'

'Well, whatever he's up to he's doing it in Wales and not on *our* patch,' Marsh reminded him.

Bill Forward still wasn't comfortable about Farrow, but took the interview file and read through it while Marsh did the same with his copy.

The door suddenly opened and Superintendent Lamb looked in. 'Oh, you're back. I looked in earlier but you were out.'

'Yes, sir. We went over to Stafford House to see Lady Pace-Warren. We haven't been back long,' he said with an innocent expression.

'How was she?' asked Lamb with concern. 'You didn't upset her, I hope.'

'No, sir. But I did have to tell her that Sir Reginald had spent Friday night in a Newcastle hotel with a woman he said was his wife.'

'Good grief. And that didn't upset her?'

'As a matter of fact it didn't appear to, no. She'd apparently suspected that he had a woman somewhere for some time. My news only served to confirm her suspicion, it seems.'

'Well, all I can say is, tread gently. We can't have the press getting hold of *that*. They'd destroy the poor woman.'

'We'll be as discreet as possible, sir.'

'Have you any leads yet?' asked Lamb.

'Nothing positive but we're following up one or two.'

'Well, don't forget. If you need an extra man I'll arrange it.'

'Thank you, sir. I won't forget.'

After Lamb had left, Marsh said, 'I liked your, "We haven't been back long." Good job you weren't too close or he might have smelt the red wine that Lady Pace-Warren *insisted* you had before we left Stafford House.' He grinned.

'Good point, Sergeant. Get me a coffee in case he comes back.'

Marsh phoned the canteen while Bill Forward carried on looking at the interviews.

Fiona and Edward had finished their lunch and moved back to the sitting room. They sat next to each other on the settee, finishing their wine.

He put his empty glass down and said, 'I really enjoyed having lunch with you. It was nice to be just the two of us.'

'I know what you mean. I can't remember the last time I was so completely at ease,' she said with a warmth in her voice.

'You must have felt like that with your husband in the beginning, surely?' said Edward.

'I can't remember ever feeling like this with him,' she said as she put her glass down. With concern, she added, 'Don't let Philippa know you and I were alone here, will you?'

'You have my word on that. She's the last person I would say anything to. She knows I was coming to see you but only for a moment. Then I was going for some lunch in the Kings Road and have a look round before going back to the Travelodge.'

'It's just that Angie saw you arrive and she will no doubt be wondering why you came. But I don't think she would cause trouble like Philippa would. It's just that I don't want my friends thinking badly of me. Not with the funeral and everything to organize. I think I shall need my friends to help get me through all that.'

'I wish I could be with you.'

'You know that's not possible. That *would* really set tongues wagging.'

'Suppose I came with Philippa?'

She gave a nervous laugh and said, 'Edward, that's out of the question. If they saw you look at me the way you're looking at me now, they would *know* you weren't there to be with the lovely Philippa.'

'Does the way I'm looking at you bother you?'

Trying not to show any emotion, she said, 'Yes. And now I think it's time you should go. And let's hope no one sees you leave, or they'll know you didn't just pop in for a moment.'

As she got up to go, he took her hand and stood beside her.

'Before I leave, I want you to know that seeing you again has been wonderful. And although I understand you wanting to be cautious, I would very much like to see you again as soon as is possible. If you would like to, that is?'

Fiona saw the look in his eyes again and, throwing caution to the wind, kissed his cheek and said, 'Yes. I would like to. Just as soon as this horrible time is over, I really would like to. I don't know why but I feel so comfortable and relaxed with you.'

He wanted desperately to kiss her lips but didn't want to spoil this new relationship. Instead, he kissed her hand and said, 'Thank your housekeeper for the lunch.'

'I will.'

As they walked into the hall and towards the front door, he stopped and gave her his card. 'This is out of date now, but the mobile number is still the same. Just in case you should want me for anything. You never know.'

She took the card and smiled. 'You never know.'

He opened the front door and looked out. 'I would rather have waited until it was dark. But I don't think there's anyone hiding in the trees with a camera.' Edward blew her a kiss and left.

She watched him leave and closed the door. Fiona knew that many men fancied her and would probably jump into bed with her given half a chance. But she had a feeling deep down that Edward was not like that and didn't want to be with her purely for sex. It was this that made her want to see him again. She looked at his card where it described him as the manager of a travel agency. And she imagined that he was an efficient and nice man in business, compared to Reggie, who could be so ruthless. Fiona had felt strangely relaxed with Edward. But now she was feeling guilty as her thoughts were brought back to the reality of the moment, and the fact that her husband had been killed in his study only the night before by persons unknown. And she was curious to know who Reggie had spent the night with in Newcastle. Now she had to face arranging his funeral, and no doubt more police investigations. She didn't want to be alone again tonight and although she had friends she could visit, she found it strange to be wishing that Edward was still there with her.

When Ken and Paul finished their game of golf, they changed and went to join their wives in the bar. Before they had a chance to order any drinks, Angie informed them of Fiona's visitor and the fact that she had invited him into the house.

'Lucky devil,' said Ken. 'She never invited *me* in when I went round.'

'When was this?' Angie asked with surprise.

'This morning just after Paul left,' he said, trying to keep a straight face.

Angie and Sheila realized they were being teased when both men started laughing.

'You should have seen your face, Sheila! You were beginning to believe him,' Paul said. 'Let's get the drinks in and sit down.'

'We thought you men might be interested, that's all,' said Angie. 'But if you don't want to be serious, fine.'

'We'd like two more gin and tonics, please,' Sheila called as the men went to the bar.

While they waited for their order, Paul lowered his voice and said to Ken, 'If Fiona invited that Edward into the house, it might have been because of the cold weather and she wanted to get him warmed up.' He grinned.

'You mustn't get me excited,' Ken chuckled. 'Not on an empty stomach.'

Paul took the two drinks for their wives and said, 'Let's go and listen to the girls' thoughts on what Fiona is up to. And try and look serious or you'll upset them.' He smiled and they made their way to the table, wondering what scandal the girls were going to come up with.

Bill Forward had just received the post mortem report on Sir Reginald Pace-Warren and was reading it out to Marsh.

'Death caused by one heavy blow to the neck with a log of wood. Time of death was between 7 and 8.15 p.m. Then it goes on with his blood type et cetera. The rest is all medical jargon.'

'The first guests arrived at about seven fifteen,' said

Marsh, checking his notes. 'So if one of *them* killed him, it had to be after that.'

'Yes. But don't let us forget the meter reader. I'd still like to know who he was, and if he did manage to get into the house, what time that was.' He put the report down and looked at the list of phone numbers that Marsh had from the phone company. 'I want you to go back to see Lady Pace-Warren in the morning and ask her if she recognizes any of these numbers. Apart from her friends, I mean. If her husband *did* receive a threatening call, we might strike lucky.'

Marsh gave a frustrated sigh. 'Why can't it be a simple case of wife shoots husband?'

'Because we're detectives, sunshine, and our job is to detect. If you were Sherlock Holmes and had those phone numbers, you'd have this case wrapped up in no time.' said Bill.

Before Marsh could reply, the door suddenly opened and Superintendent Lamb walked in.

'We just received a 999 and uniform went to see what it was about and found the body of a woman in her flat. She had been beaten over the head. The victim was on your list as one of the guests at Stafford House last night. A Philippa Pane,' Lamb informed them.

'We interviewed her last night!' exclaimed Bill.

'She was the mixer. A proper troublemaker, we thought,' said Marsh.

'The uniform lads said she had a jack of clubs tucked into her cleavage when they found her. That sounds a bit odd,' said Lamb.

'That was the card of the murderer in the game they were playing last night, sir. We all wondered where that was.'

'Well, you'd better get over there and see if this woman's death *is* connected with the Pace-Warren case. The scenes of crime officer and forensics have been informed and are on their way. Call in to my office and I'll give you the address.'

Marsh said, 'I've got it in my notebook, sir.'

'Well, off you go and good luck. Let me know as soon as you have anything. I want to be kept informed all the way with this case.'

'Do we know who called 999, sir?' Bill asked.

'Yes, her neighbour. A Mr Neville. He heard someone shout, "Take that, you bitch" in the adjoining flat apparently. Then her door slammed shut and he heard someone running down the stairs,' the superintendent said as he left.

'Well, there goes our quiet Sunday in the office,' Bill sighed. 'I wonder if Miss Pane had poked her nose into Pace-Warren's death a bit too far for her own good?'

'And scared his killer into keeping her quiet, permanently, you mean?' Marsh asked.

'Yes. Well, let's get over there and see what we can find out.'

Kelvin Mansions did not give the impression of being a very salubrious place, with the outside paintwork looking in desperate need of renewing. Apartment 43 was so cluttered up it was more like an auction room than a place to live. Bill could see why Edward King found the thought of him staying there so ludicrous. Bill and Marsh put on protective clothing and checked doors and windows. There was no sign of a break-in so they went into the kitchen, where Philippa Pane's body was lying on the imitation tiled vinyl floor, being examined by the pathologist.

'What have we got here?' asked Bill.

'It appears to be fairly straightforward. She was beaten over the head with something quite solid. The wound on the skull suggests something round and smooth. Forensic think it might be the old wooden rolling pin in the bag over there.'

Bill picked up the plastic bag from the worktop and looked at the rolling pin. 'I can't see any blood on it,' he said.

'The killer must have worn gloves,' said the doctor. 'It looks as though she was killed with a single blow and died within the last hour or so. We'll know more precisely after I've done the post mortem. Oh and there was a playing card put down her cleavage, which seems a bit odd. Forensic put it in a bag and took it to the other room.'

'We know about the card. It was possibly to tell us that the person who killed Sir Reginald last night is the same person who committed this one.'

'A sort of calling card?'

'Something like that, yes. Is there anything else I should know?' Bill asked.

'I don't think so. Unless you want her, I'll get her taken to the morgue.'

'I can't think of anything we want her for. Can you, Marsh?'

'No. Her hands look clean enough. No sign that she might have struggled or scratched her assailant, is there, Doctor?'

'It looks as though she was hit from behind without putting up any resistance at all. Just like your Saturday night victim.'

'Then it must have been someone she knew and opened the door to. Someone she felt safe to be alone with,' Marsh said.

Bill looked at his watch, which read 4.46. 'And she was killed around an hour ago. So it was between three and three forty. Is that correct, Doc?'

'As near as I can tell,' the doctor answered. 'I'll let you know for certain as soon as I can. And now I'll be off, unless there's anything else?'

'There is just one thing, Doctor,' said Bill.

'What's that?'

'Can we stop meeting this often? My wife will think I've got a woman somewhere.'

The doctor smiled and pointed to Philippa Pane's body. 'You *have now*. Goodbye.'

Bill gave a friendly wave as the doctor left the kitchen. 'Let's go and look at the card they found on her. Then we can see if it matches the one from the pack they had at Stafford House.'

They walked through to the sitting room where the forensic photographer had just finished getting various shots of the room. Another man was dusting the door for fingerprints. Bill picked up a plastic bag from the table. In it was the jack of clubs card and a small pocket diary.

'Have these been checked for prints?' he asked.

'Yes, but there's nothing on the card. They must have worn gloves. And what's written in the diary is a bit like this room, a jumbled-up mess.'

'Thanks,' Bill said, and took it to the bedroom, where the scenes of crime officer was busy looking through a chest of drawers.

'Hello, Inspector. There's nothing much here except sweaters and underwear. But there was a small case under the bed that contained an assortment of sexual aids. Real kinky, they are. Do you want to see them?'

'Not unless one of them could be the murder weapon,' Bill said with a straight face.

Marsh smiled to himself and asked, 'Is it OK to take the playing card with us? Forensics couldn't get any prints from it.'

'We need to check if it matches a pack at Stafford House,' Bill explained. 'And I'd like to take a look at the diary too.'

'If forensics say it's OK. But make sure they go back to them when you've finished. You know the drill.'

Bill put the card and diary in his pocket and had a look around the flat. He went back to the kitchen and looked down at Philippa's body again. As he was doing so, the telephone in the hall rang and Marsh picked up the receiver. 'Hello.'

Fiona was obviously surprised to hear a man's voice. 'Is that *you*, Edward?'

'No. This is Detective Sergeant Marsh. May I ask who it is calling?'

'Hello, Sergeant. This is Fiona Pace-Warren. Is Philippa there?'

'I'm afraid not, m'lady'.

When Bill Forward heard who it was calling, he came into the hall and signalled that he would talk to her.

'Is something wrong, Sergeant?' Fiona asked.

'Inspector Forward is here, ma'am. He'd like a word with you,' said Marsh, handing Bill the receiver.

'This is DI Forward, ma'am. I have some bad news, I'm afraid.'

'Why? What's happened?'

'Miss Pane was found dead here about an hour ago.'

Fiona was obviously shocked. 'Dead! But I only spoke to her a little while ago. She phoned and said she thought she knew who my husband's murderer was. But as she didn't want to tell me on the phone, or come to the house, could we meet somewhere? I told her I would call her back and arrange where and what time we could meet. To be honest, I thought she was just seeking attention as usual. Poor Philippa. What was it, a heart attack?'

'No, ma'am. She was beaten over the head by someone.'

'Oh my God!' Fiona gasped.

'Would it be convenient to come and see you? It's important. There are some things I need to know that I think you can help me with,' said Bill.

Fiona was trying to come to terms with the news of Philippa's death as she replied, 'I shall wait here at the house for you.'

'Thank you. I must ask you not to discuss this with anyone else until we have spoken, ma'am. Not even your house-keeper. You understand?'

'Yes … Of course.' When the inspector hung up, Fiona was shaking and went to get herself a glass of brandy, wishing Edward was still with her.

After he rang off, Bill went with Marsh to see the neigh-bour, Mr Neville, who repeated what he had told the constables when they responded to his 999 call. But he couldn't be sure whether the voice he heard shouting 'Take that, you bitch' was a man or woman. And it transpired that he didn't actually see the person leaving Philippa's apart-ment and running down the stairs. Inspector Forward saw no point in interviewing him further and after thanking him, returned with Marsh back to Stafford House.

Fiona had managed to calm down by the time Inspector Forward and Sergeant Marsh arrived. They went into the sitting room and sat down.

'I can't get over someone actually killing poor Philippa,' said Fiona. 'I know she liked to gossip but she was a lonely soul and in a way I felt sorry for her.'

'Her friend Edward King will no doubt be shocked,' said Bill.

'Yes, he will. I thought it was him when I heard your sergeant answer her phone,' Fiona said. 'You said I wasn't to tell anyone about her being killed. Not even Mrs Romaine. Why is that, Inspector? Surely one way or another, everyone will soon know? Won't they?'

'I didn't want you telling anyone because we still believe that it was someone who was in this house last night that killed your husband. That same person may have killed Miss Pane, and until we find them, you yourself may be in danger.'

90

'You can't be serious.'

'Yes, I am. And for that reason, I want to give you some protection. I shall have a female officer stay with you until we apprehend the person responsible for these deaths.'

Fiona was trying to take this in and got up to pour herself another brandy. 'I cannot believe this is happening. Do you think Philippa really did know who killed my husband and that's why she was killed?'

'It looks that way.'

'That's so scary. If your PC stays here, will I still be able to have my friends visit without her having to sit with us all the time?'

'Yes, of course. But it's important they know she's around and could be with you in an instant,' Bill told her.

'I understand that, Inspector.'

Bill gave Marsh a nod and the sergeant made a call to arrange for a woman police officer to come to the house and remain with Fiona.

'One of us will stay with you until the officer arrives,' Bill told her. 'Can you let me see the design on the back of the cards you distributed for your murder game?'

Fiona thought for a moment. 'They're in the drawer.' She put down her brandy glass and went to fetch the pack of cards from a bureau. 'The back of the cards are blue and white squares, Inspector. Is that important?'

'A jack of clubs was put on Miss Pane's body. And it's the same design as you've just described. May I see?'

'That's the card we thought was lost!' said Fiona. 'And there I was, wondering why the person who had chosen it hadn't put it back with the others,' she said, passing Bill the pack.

'They placed it on her body instead,' said Bill.

'How sick!' Fiona said with a cold shudder. 'That's horrible.'

Bill went through the pack of cards and said, 'It's from the same pack all right and it's the only one that's missing.' He put the card found on the body back in his pocket. 'Does Miss Pane have any relatives that we can notify?'

'I don't think she has. Her gentleman friend might know.'

'Does this man have a name?' Bill asked.

'It's Conway. Robert Conway. He lives locally. But I don't know his phone number,' she said.

Bill turned to Marsh. 'See if he's in her diary.'

'Right,' said Marsh, and he took the diary from Bill.

'My party was meant to be a fun evening.' Fiona said. 'But now there are two funerals to arrange. And you believe someone at my party deliberately killed them, don't you?'

'It's the only logical explanation we have at the moment. And I'm afraid there might be a delay with the funeral, ma'am.'

'I don't understand.'

Bill tried to explain, without making the situation sound too complicated. 'The lawyers for the accused may not accept the post mortem report, and insist on an independent one. In that case there could be a further delay.'

'Oh God, this is becoming more of a nightmare every day.'

'I'm sorry, ma'am, but that's the way it is, I'm afraid. You can be sure we shall catch this killer as soon as we can. And I would still like to look at your husband's business records. Is there anywhere you could look? Somewhere he might have put them, other than in his study?'

'I really can't think of anywhere,' Fiona told him. 'But if you want to search the house yourself, I have no objection. I'll help you if you would like me to.'

'Thank you, ma'am. It will give us something to do while we wait for the woman constable to arrive.'

They got up, and checked the bureau drawers and

cupboard. Then Bill and Fiona went to the dining room next door. Satisfied there were no places to keep files or records there, he decided to go up to the bedrooms. They had just finished and were on the way downstairs again when he had a sudden idea and was annoyed with himself for not thinking of it before.

'Can I have the keys to your husband's car, please, ma'am?'

Fiona had to think for a moment. 'I expect they're in his coat. I'll get them for you.' She went to the cloakroom and took the keys from his coat pocket, then went back to Bill.

'Here they are, Inspector. I don't want to look in the car. I felt funny looking at his coat just now. Do you mind?'

'I understand, ma'am.' Bill took the keys and went to the Mercedes that was parked in the garage. He searched the boot and the interior but found no files or records. In the glove compartment he found a piece of paper with a phone number on it. He recognized the Newcastle area code and decided to play a hunch and dialled the number on his mobile. A woman's voice answered. 'Hello.'

'Who am I speaking to?' asked Bill in a friendly voice.

'Who is that calling?' she asked.

'This is the MacCann hotel. When you were here with your husband on Friday night, Mr Carrington left some papers and I wondered if he left them by mistake or wanted them thrown away.'

The woman had clearly been caught off guard. 'Oh! I'll tell him.' Then she quickly added, 'No. It's all right. Throw them away.'

'Very well, madam.' Bill rang off, feeling pleased his hunch had paid off and that he'd found the bogus wife. Putting the piece of paper in his pocket, he locked the car and returned to the house where Marsh told him he'd found Robert Conway's phone number and left a voicemail for him to call.

Bill told him to go back to the office while he waited for the constable.

He only had to wait a few minutes after Marsh left before Constable Weston, a woman in her late twenties arrived and parked in the drive. Bill gave her his instructions and once he was sure Lady Pace-Warren felt safer and seemed more relaxed, he returned to his office.

Fiona was glad to have someone with her but wished the constable was not wearing her uniform.

'What do I call you?' asked Fiona. 'Constable?'

'No, ma'am.' She smiled. 'My name is Katherine, but everyone calls me Kate. And by the way, DI Forward wants people to know there's a police officer here, so it's OK if you tell them.'

'Yes, he explained that to me. I should like to phone my friends soon and tell them of someone else's death.'

'Please carry on doing what you want to. I shall try not to be in your way. But could you show me round the house first? I'd like to see my room and get my bearings.'

'Yes, of course. I thought you'd like to be in the single bedroom. I think you will be comfortable there,' Fiona said, and led the way upstairs. Kate Weston finished her tour of the house and began to settle into her room. While Fiona had the chance to be alone, she made her first phone call. To her it was an important one.

Edward King answered his mobile and was pleased to hear his caller's voice.

'Hello, Edward. It's Fiona. You told me to call if I wanted you for anything.'

His voice was warm and sexy as he asked, 'And *do* you? Want me for anything, I mean?'

'Yes, I do. I want you to be with me. In fact, I wish you hadn't left after our lovely lunch together. And now I have something very important to tell you, but not on the phone. Can you come here, rather than meet somewhere?' she asked, hoping for an affirmative reply.

'I'll be there just as soon as I can get a taxi.'

Fiona felt better when she knew he was on his way. And although she was well aware that she could be getting herself involved in an awkward situation, she didn't care. She just wanted to experience the pleasure of Edward's company again. While she waited for him to arrive, she decided to make some other phone calls and get them over with.

CHAPTER TEN

Andrew Davis was shocked to hear about Philippa but Janet was more philosophical about it and showed little sympathy.

'Women like that dreadful Pane woman are asking for trouble when they go around spreading rumours about people. She was a mischievous bitch and, although I wouldn't wish it on any human being, I'm not surprised she got her comeuppance in the end.'

'But she was murdered, for Christ's sake. Surely the poor woman didn't deserve *that*, Janet.'

'No. You're right. I'm sorry. It's just that you men are all too busy fancying Fiona to see what an unfaithful bastard Reggie was and what a troublemaking bitch Philippa is. I mean was. Although I have to be honest and say she did have Reggie sussed out. But we girls knew he was getting his leg over with someone.'

Andrew threw up his arms in despair. 'Now you're doing just what you accused Philippa of. That's being mischievous.'

'Oh, charming. Thank you.'

'Well, you are. And by the way, Fiona has a policewoman staying with her. So if we go round there, and you see a woman with a truncheon in her hand, behave yourself or you might feel the full weight of the law descend on you.'

'Very funny, I'm sure.' Janet was thoughtful for a moment. 'Are you serious about a policewoman staying there?'

'Yes.'

'I must admit, I never thought of Fiona needing protection. Did you?'

'No, I didn't. But I suppose with Philippa's murder coming on top of Reggie's like that, the police may have information that we don't know about,' Andrew said. 'Anyway, I think you should go and see Fiona when you've got a minute. After all, you're supposed to be her friend.'

Janet became slightly uncomfortable as she said, 'Yes. Yes of course I must.'

After Bill Forward had given his update on the case to Superintendent Lamb, he went back to his office and informed Marsh about his chat to the woman in Newcastle.

'What happens when she tries to contact Sir Reginald?' asked Marsh.'

'She'd try his mobile and leave a voicemail for him to call. When she gets no reply from him she might chance ringing the house. If a female business associate calls that number we'll know soon enough. She didn't appear to have a Geordie accent, so I don't think she's a local. It would be nice to know who she is though. We could ask the Newcastle lads to find out. If we give them the phone number it wouldn't take them long. Give them a call.'

Marsh dialled the number and requested the Newcastle police's assistance in his murder inquiry. When he'd finished the call, Marsh asked, 'Who's the PC they sent over to Stafford House?'

'Katherine Weston. You probably know her. Nice-looking

woman. Understood exactly what we want and will no doubt keep a firm eye on everything. Her ladyship will feel safer with her in the house.'

'I bet her ladyship's friends will be calling round now that she's got a lady police officer there, just out of curiosity.'

'It's the friend who *doesn't* want to call because there's a police officer there that I'd be interested in,' said Bill. 'I just wish we had a suspect rather than twelve people who may or may not be the one we want.'

'It's eleven, not counting her ladyship,' Marsh corrected him.

'You're forgetting the meter reader, Sergeant. And we mustn't forget *him*, must we?'

Fiona heard the bell ring and, hoping it was Edward, she hurried to open the door. Her smile, when she saw him standing there, made it obvious how delighted she was to see him. His expression turned from happiness to anxiety as he saw the policewoman appear in the background.

'What is it, Fiona? What's happened?' he asked with concern.

She quickly introduced him to Kate and tried to put his mind at rest. 'Inspector Forward didn't want me to be alone. So Kate will be staying with me for a day or two. Give me your coat and go into the sitting room. I'll get some ice and we'll have a drink. I think we both need one.' Then, turning to Kate, she said, 'Come into the kitchen and help yourself to tea or coffee. I'll show you where everything is.'

'Thank you, ma'am. Then I'll be in the breakfast room if you need me,' said Kate.

Fiona took Kate on a quick tour of the kitchen, then got some ice from the fridge and went back to the living room and Edward. She was not looking forward to telling him about

Philippa's death. She poured him a whisky and herself a brandy, and then sat next to him on the settee.

'Now, what's this "something" you wouldn't tell me about on the phone?' he asked. 'Is it something to do with that policewoman being here? I nearly had a fit when I saw her. I thought something terrible had happened.'

'It has. There's been another murder. It's someone who was here at the party.'

'Christ! Who was it?'

'Brace yourself, Edward. It was Philippa.'

'You're joking!'

'No. No, I'm not. She was beaten over the head by someone.'

'But why would somebody want to kill Philippa?'

'The police think she was close to naming the killer. She was convinced she knew who it was. In fact, she wanted to meet me and tell me who she thought it was. Now you can understand why Inspector Forward wanted me to have police protection. If the killer thought Philippa had told me their name, I could be in danger too. That's why I wanted you here with me,' she said. 'I feel safe with you. I don't know why.'

He put his drink down and, with both arms around her, pulled her to him and held her tight. 'Perhaps you're on the rebound after hearing that your husband had been staying with another woman,' he said.

Fiona closed her eyes and quietly said, 'Whatever it is, it's very nice having you here.'

'I'll stay with you as long as you want me to,' he whispered. Then unable to resist any longer, Edward kissed her passionately, and Fiona responded, her tongue moving closer to his until they were exploring each other. His hand moved slowly towards her breast and she knew she would be unable to resist if he went any further. As he was about to undo the buttons on her blouse, the front doorbell rang. She quickly got up and made sure she looked decent. 'Stay there. Hopefully, whoever it is won't stay.' She gave Edward a warm smile and left to answer the door.

Katherine stood by the breakfast room, waiting to see who the visitor was. When Fiona opened the door, she was surprised to see Sara Wilson standing there, holding a bouquet of flowers. 'We thought these might help cheer you up,' she said. 'David has a surgery. Otherwise he'd be here.'

Fiona gratefully accepted the bouquet and said, 'That is very kind of you, Sara. Thank you. Come in.'

Sara caught sight of Katherine as she went back into the breakfast room. 'I'm sorry. I didn't know you had the police here,' Sara said with surprise.

'Oh, of course you didn't. I tried ringing to tell you earlier but there was no reply. So you don't know about Philippa.'

'Know what about Philippa?'

'She's been murdered as well.'

'You're not serious!'

'Yes, I am. Come to the kitchen while I put these in water and I'll tell you about it.'

Edward could hear Sara's voice and hoped she wouldn't be staying. He finished his drink, wondering if he and Fiona would ever get the chance to be alone.

Fiona had given Sara full details on the Philippa saga and then convinced her that she needed to be alone and sort out some papers. After thanking her again for the flowers, she saw Sara out and returned to Edward.

'I'm sorry,' she said. 'I got rid of her as soon as I could. But it was kind of her to call. She brought me some lovely flowers.'

'So I gathered,' he said.

She saw his empty glass and asked, 'Would you like another drink?'

'What I would really like is to pick up from where we left off,' he said softly. 'But I don't think it's possible.'

'Why?' she whispered teasingly.

'Because that blasted doorbell will probably ring again.' He smiled. 'Or your housekeeper will arrive unexpectedly. Or your bodyguard will come bursting in, threatening me with her truncheon. So I think I'll have that drink now. And then I want to talk to you. And I mean seriously talk.'

Fiona could tell he wasn't joking and after she refreshed his drink, sat next to him, wondering what he was going to say.

Edward took a large swig of whisky, which almost drained his glass. Then he put the glass on the table and turned to her.

'You know that men fancy you and would jump into bed with you given half a chance. But you must also know that when I kissed you before your visitor arrived, it was more than just a sexual urge. And the way you responded I think it was the same for you. Last night, in the cloakroom, it was different. I was enjoying the thrill of being alone with the girl I used to fancy so much. But now, after all you've been through, I really am beginning to care about you. I don't think you should stay in this house tonight. The effect of what happened yesterday hasn't hit you yet. You should go somewhere where you'll be safe. I don't want to sound possessive, but I'm becoming very fond of you, Fiona, and I couldn't bear it if anything happened to you.' He took her hand and with a warm smile added, 'I don't want to lose you. Not now that I've found you again.'

She saw the sincere, caring look in his eyes and said, 'It's only tonight I've got to get through. Mrs Romaine will be here in the morning and things will get back to normal.'

'You want me to stay with you until the morning. Is that what you're saying?' he asked.

'I wish we weren't here in this house, but somewhere miles away, staying in a nice hotel together where I could feel like a real person again. That's what I would like.'

Edward gave a quizzical look and asked, 'What do mean by "a real person"?'

She put her hand on his and gave a loving smile. 'To feel like I do now. To be with someone who really cares about *me*, and not just a young, attractive woman he needs, in order to impress his friends and business associates. It's funny, but I used to enjoy being a titled lady at first. I was young and it made me feel very special. Now I just want to be happy again.'

'Forgive my ignorance, but what happens to your title now that your husband is dead?' asked Edward.

'I keep the name and title unless I marry again.'

'So if I ever proposed to you I'd be turned down or you'd be just plain Mrs? That's a hypothetical question, of course,' he said with a smile that teased her.

'Perhaps you should ask me that question again, when it *isn't* hypothetical,' Fiona replied with an equally teasing smile.

Despite the temptation to kiss her, Edward tried to control his emotions as he said, 'Much as I want to, you know I can't stay with you tonight, don't you? You cannot afford to have your character destroyed by having me stay the night. Even if I slept on the settee, no one would believe we hadn't shared a bed together. And I don't want that sort of gossip going round about us. You'd never live it down.'

'I don't want to be alone, Edward. I keep trying to push the memory of seeing Reggie in the study right out of my mind. But I can't. I really feel safe when I'm with you. And now with Philippa dead, I'm frightened.'

Edward put his arm around her and was wondering what

he could do when the phone rang. Fiona answered it and heard Inspector Forward.

'Sorry to bother you, ma'am. I'm just ringing to see if you are all right and how you're getting on with PC Weston.'

'To tell you the truth, Inspector, I haven't seen much of her. I've had visitors since she arrived. But she seems very nice and she's settled into her room.' Edward signalled that he wished to speak with the inspector. 'Just a moment, Inspector. Somebody wants to talk to you.' She passed Edward the handset with a look of curiosity.

'Hello, Inspector. This is Edward King.'

'Hello, sir. Can I help you?'

'Yes, I'd like your advice, Inspector. I don't want to leave Fiona alone tonight. And she would feel safer if I stayed. But I don't want to ruin her reputation by staying, even though I would be discreet. But we would like to know what you think we should do.'

'My only concern is for her safety, sir. If her ladyship wants you to stay with her, that is her personal wish and I see no reason why I should object. After all, you are both adults and what you do in private is none of my business. But if you stay you must let PC Weston know of your intention.'

'Yes, of course. Thank you, Inspector.' He smiled and gave Fiona the thumbs-up.

'Just one thing, though.' Bill said.

'What's that, Inspector?'

'It might be more discreet if you left *early* in the morning. Now can I have a word with her ladyship, please?'

'Yes, of course.' Edward handed Fiona the phone. 'He wants a word with you.'

Fiona wondered what Bill wanted now. 'Yes, Inspector?'

'Does the name Karen Watts mean anything to you, ma'am?'

'No. Should it?'

'I only ask because it's the name of the woman who stayed with your husband in Newcastle. I thought she might be a business associate.'

'The name means nothing to me, Inspector.'

'Well, thank you, ma'am. Have a good evening and try not to worry about anything. You'll have PC Weston there, and Mr King will be staying with you tonight, so you'll be quite safe. I'll be in touch. Good night, ma'am.'

Fiona put the phone down with a look of surprise. 'He said you were staying with me tonight. He even sounded pleased.'

Edward squeezed her hand. 'You've got to hand it to our police. They're very efficient.' Then he added with a smile, 'If any visitors call, PC Weston can tell them you're out. And by the way, we've got to tell her I'm staying. Do you want to do it or shall I?'

'I shall tell her in a minute,' Fiona said. 'But first, come here.' She pulled him towards her and gave him a long and passionate kiss.

Sergeant Marsh had heard his inspector's conversation with Edward King and gave him a look of disbelief.

'Did I just hear you give your encouragement for them to sleep together? And say that with King there she'll be safe?'

'You did, yes.'

'Are you forgetting that King is a suspect for her husband's murder, sir?'

'No, I am not, Sergeant.'

'So he's going to be alone with her, but you tell her she'll be quite safe, despite the fact that he might be a murderer. I don't understand.'

Bill Forward became impatient. 'Oh, come on Sergeant, think. If King *is* the murderer, he's hardly likely to kill her when he's the only person in the house apart from a police constable, now is he? And there is another possibility that you may not have considered. It's something that came to mind when I spoke to her ladyship just now.'

'What's that?'

'Suppose *she* planned to kill her husband and that the dinner party was just a cover. She wouldn't be afraid to spend the night alone with King then, would she? Because she'd know he wasn't the murderer.'

'But if your theory is right, why was Philippa Pane killed?' Marsh asked.

'According to her ladyship, Miss Pane telephoned to tell her that she knew who'd killed Sir Reginald, and asked to meet her to discuss it, probably intending to blackmail her. In which case her ladyship would get scared and have to shut her up before she could make it public, wouldn't she?'

'Oh, come on, sir. How could she go to the apartment, kill the woman and get back here again without someone seeing her? She's far too attractive to go anywhere without being noticed. Besides, the housekeeper would know if she'd left the house.'

'You're probably right,' said Bill with frustration. 'It was just an idea. But someone committed a murder on my patch and I want to know who it was. So far, we've got a phoney meter reader that Mrs Romaine can't describe, and the name of a woman who spent the night with Sir Reginald in Newcastle, but bugger all else. Let's have another look at that list of guests again. Logic, plus my gut feeling, tells me that it had to be one of them.'

'I agree. That's my gut feeling too.'

They sat quietly studying their copies of the guest list, each hoping to come up with something tangible in the way of a lead that would move their investigation forward.

*

Fiona told Kate that her male companion would be staying over, and invited her to join them for something to eat rather than be alone. After looking at the many meals the freezer and refrigerator had to offer, they all chose the easiest one to prepare, a vegetable quiche.

As they enjoyed the meal, they had a friendly conversation, during which the murder was not discussed. It was just after they had finished eating that the telephone rang. Fiona lifted the receiver and heard Janet Davis's voice on the other end.

'Hello, Fiona. It's Janet. How are you?'

'Not too bad, thank you, Janet.'

'That's good. I'm ringing to see if you'd like some company. Only I could come over for a while this evening if you want me to. Andrew is busy working to a deadline and I'm sure he'd be glad to get rid of me.'

'That's very kind of you, but I have got some company, so I'm fine.' Kate indicated for herself to be mentioned. 'Actually she's a woman police officer. And she'll be staying with me tonight.'

'Oh yes, Andrew did tell me. She's nice, is she?'

'Very. As a matter of fact we've just had a meal together. And now we are just having a drink and a chat before having an early night.'

'So you'll have Mrs Romaine *and* your police lady with you tonight. Well, as long as you're all right.'

'Yes, I'm fine, really. But it's kind of you to be concerned. I really appreciate it.'

'Isn't that what friends are for? I expect Andrew will look in on you tomorrow. Just to make sure you're OK. I'll leave you in peace now. Good night, Fiona. Sleep well.'

'Thank you Janet. Good night.' She put the receiver down

and said, 'She thinks Mrs Romaine is here as well. I hope she doesn't find out that she isn't or she'll wonder what's going on.'

Kate saw the awkward look that passed between Fiona and Edward and decided it was time to thank them for the food and their company then leave them alone.

When Kate had gone, Fiona asked Edward, 'Did I sound all right on the phone? Only I felt like a naughty schoolgirl.'

'Well, I wasn't one hundred per cent comfortable at first, with that police uniform sitting opposite me. But after a while I forgot she was a police officer. She's very nice.'

'I hope you're not beginning to fancy her,' Fiona joked.

Edward smiled and whispered, 'Why don't we go upstairs and then you'll know who I fancy?' He took her hand and without saying a word, Fiona went with him to the bedroom.

Jane Forward had given her husband an evening meal and watched him sit back in his armchair and close his eyes.

'Why don't you have an early night for a change?' she said. 'You haven't had a break since your last case and if you aren't careful you'll be too tired to do *anything*. You mustn't overdo things, Bill.'

He opened his eyes and gave a nod. 'I know. It's just that I've got too many suspects. I can't seem to think straight and it annoys me.'

'Take one of my tablets, they'll help you sleep. Go on. Off you go. A good night's rest is all you need to recharge your batteries.'

Bill went without resisting, hoping that he would feel more refreshed in the morning.

CHAPTER ELEVEN

Fiona was in a deep sleep when Edward's wristwatch alarm buzzed. It was almost 6 a.m. He quietly washed and dressed, then left and picked up a taxi in the Kings Road.

By the time Fiona woke it was gone seven. She looked at the empty space in the bed next to her and cuddled Edward's pillow, wishing he was still there and that their night together hadn't ended. It had been the most exciting night she had ever experienced. And having slept with another man so soon after Reggie's murder, she was surprised that she didn't feel any sense of guilt.

After having a bath she dressed and made the bed before going down to have breakfast. When she got to the kitchen, she was surprised to see Mrs Romaine tidying up.

'Good morning,' Fiona said. 'I didn't expect you this early.'

'I didn't sleep very well,' she replied. 'So I thought I'd come in and see if I could do anything. Did your visitor enjoy the lunch I made for you yesterday?'

'Yes, we both did. It was lovely, thank you, and by the way ...'

'Yes?'

'I slept in the guest room last night. And there's a lady staying in the single room. She's a policewoman and she'll be here for a day or two. It's the inspector's orders. He wants to make sure I'm safe.'

'Safe?' Mrs Romaine said with surprise. 'Safe from what?'

'Oh, of course, you don't know. Philippa Pane has been murdered.'

Mrs Romaine looked shocked as she said, 'Good Lord!'

'Apparently she knew who the killer was and they wanted to shut her up before she could tell anyone. That's what the police think anyway. And that's why Kate, she's the PC is here. She's a sort of bodyguard.'

'But why would *you* be in danger? I don't understand.'

'Because Philippa phoned and told me she thought she knew who Reggie's killer was, but wouldn't tell me on the phone. She wanted to meet somewhere to tell me but we never did meet.'

'Well, now I understand why the police are worried about *your* safety. They're quite right. You mustn't be alone, especially at night.'

Fiona decided to be honest with her. 'I wasn't alone last night. Mr King stayed with me. With the inspector's approval, let me add. And although Kate knows, nobody else does.'

Before Mrs Romaine could comment, Kate walked into the kitchen.

'I thought I heard voices,' she said.

'Kate. This is my housekeeper, Mrs Romaine.'

'Pleased to meet you,' said Kate.

'Likewise,' said Mrs Romaine with a smile. 'May I get you ladies some breakfast?'

'That would be nice,' said Fiona. 'I'll have some toast and coffee, please. What about you, Kate?'

'The same for me, please,' said Kate, smiling.

'We'll have it in the breakfast room,' Fiona said.

Mrs Romaine gave an affirmative nod as Kate and Fiona left the kitchen.

When they were alone, Fiona asked, 'Did you sleep all right?'

'Like a log,' said Kate. 'That bed is very comfortable. In fact, the whole room is very conducive to relaxation.'

'I'm glad you were OK. And by the way, I told Mrs Romaine that Edward stayed last night. She won't say anything and I don't want her thinking I'm behaving secretively behind her back. It would create a bad atmosphere.'

'I agree. I didn't hear him go. It must have been very early.'

'It was after seven when I woke up and he'd gone by then,' said Fiona. Then she asked, 'Do you think it was awful of me to be with Edward last night after all that has happened, and me still officially a married woman, I mean? Tell me the truth.'

'Well, you couldn't have been very happy in your marriage or you wouldn't have done what you did.'

'No, I wasn't. In fact, I found out that Reggie was spending the night before my party in a Newcastle hotel with a woman he said was his wife. That was what really hurt. It might sound a horrible thing to say, but when I heard that, I wasn't even sorry he was dead. In truth, I suppose I've been living a lie for a very long time. All my friends guessed he was sleeping around but I think they assumed that I was unaware of it. They probably even felt sorry for me. I needed Edward last night. He made me feel cared for and I wanted that. It's funny, but I don't feel ashamed at all. Can you understand that?'

Kate gave an understanding smile but made no comment because just then Mrs Romaine came in with their breakfast.

Bill Forward was glad he had taken Jane's advice and gone to bed early. The pill had worked and he'd slept soundly until seven o'clock. When he got to the office it was just after eight o'clock. He had been there over half an hour when Sergeant Marsh arrived, surprised to see Bill at his desk.

'Good morning, sir.'

'Is it still morning? And there I was thinking it's time to go home.'

'You obviously had a good night's rest. I wonder if Edward King and her ladyship did,' Marsh said with a grin.

'Give her ladyship a call and *ask* her. Better still, ring his mobile and ask *him*.' Bill gave a look of despair. 'Now let's get down to business, can we? I was going through one or two of these interviews you made a note of on Saturday evening. As far as I can see, they were mostly in the dark during the game, so none of them can be certain who was with them. For instance, Paul Robson said he was hiding in a wardrobe. But he didn't say which room. Then he asked his wife where she was and she said, "I was with a couple beside the bed in Fiona's room. I think one of them was the man with Philippa." Well, we know it wasn't Edward King, because he was in the downstairs cloakroom with her ladyship. So I'd like to talk to the Robsons again and see if they've had second thoughts as to who they might have been with Saturday night.'

'Good idea. Paul Robson works from home. Do you want me to see if he's there?'

'Yes. Let's see if we can get moving on this case today. I've also been thinking about Philippa Pane being hit with a rolling pin. Unless it was the nearest thing for the killer to pick up, what does a rolling pin suggest to you? I don't mean pastry making.'

'As a weapon, you mean.'

'Yes.'

'Something a woman would use?' said Marsh. 'I did wonder

about that. But if she really did know the name of the killer, she's not likely to let them in, is she?'

'Mr Neville wasn't sure whether the voice he heard shouting "Take that, you bitch" was a man or a woman. And it could easily have been a woman that used a log to kill Sir Reginald. We proved that a woman could easily have hit him with one of those logs. Remember that,' Bill reminded him. 'And having met Philippa Pane, she might have been saying she knew the name of his killer just to get attention to herself.'

'And died for nothing, you mean?'

'It's a thought.'

'Is there anything in her diary?'

'She doesn't often name people but uses initials a lot. That forensics chap was right when he said it was a jumbled mess. It's full of hieroglyphics. I want you to have a look at August and see if anything comes to mind.'

He passed Marsh the diary and watched for his reaction.

'I see what you mean about hieroglyphics. How does anyone make sense out of this?' He continued scrutinizing the pages and double checked one page again. 'Hang on. Did you mean this bit on August 31st?' He read it aloud. '"Went Dorking. Saw R + SW in car. Skirt up. Not seen."'

'That's the bit, yes. Anything strike you?'

'Apart from her bloody awful writing, nothing special. Should it?'

'Well, what do you think she means by "R + SW in car. Skirt up. Not seen"?' Bill asked him.

Marsh looked at the page again and said, 'She was with her man friend, R. That's probably Robert Conway. There was a strong wind. SW. Her skirt blew up but nobody saw it. Not seen. What do you think it means?'

'You're probably right, Marsh. What you just said never

occurred to me. Perhaps I'm getting too suspicious in my old age. I thought R and SW could be Reggie and Sara Wilson in a car and her skirt was pulled up. But they didn't see Philippa Pane watching them.'

Marsh laughed. 'Sir Reginald having it off in a car with the doctor's wife! You've got to be joking. Why would they do it in a car at Dorking, when they could stay in a hotel?'

'Like I said, you are probably right. But do something for your elderly, suspicious superior, would you?'

'What's that?'

'Have a look at the 7th and 14th September, and tell me what you think she was saying on those dates.'

Marsh turned the pages of the diary and read the entry for Friday September 7th. '"Went Dorking. Saw SW leave WHH. Hurried to car, left. R did same. Something going on."' Marsh then looked at Friday September 14th and read, '"R + SW at it again. D would go mad." But she doesn't say where in this entry. I see what you mean, though. If it *was* Sara Wilson she was referring to, then D could be for Doctor or David.'

'Yes. And it looks as though they had a regular get-together every Friday. At least for a while they did.'

'But who or what does she mean by WHH?' asked Marsh.

'There's a hotel off Dorking High Street called the White Hart. Jane and I used to stop there for a coffee and sandwich on our way to her mother's in Worthing. So Philippa Pane could have seen them when she was shopping. Where she saw them at it in the car we don't know. Maybe they couldn't get a day room for a *business* meeting, who knows? But if they really were having it away, she would be right about Doctor David going mad if he found out.'

'And he was one person who could go into the study and not look suspicious. And he'd know exactly how and where to hit Sir Reginald with a log,' said Marsh.

'Yes, interesting isn't it? Now see if Paul Robson is at home and we can pay him a visit.'

'What are we going to do about the doctor?'

'Tread carefully. That's what we're going to do. I want to give that some careful thought.'

Marsh got through to Paul Robson and arranged to interview him in half an hour's time. Bill Forward and Marsh went through the other interviews to see if any of them wanted checking again. Bill looked at David Wilson's statement and read it to Marsh.

'He said that Sir Reginald must have died instantly and that his wife, Sara, was upstairs looking after Fiona. So if he was going to kill anyone, why not his wife if he'd found out she was being unfaithful. Why kill the man?'

'I don't know,' Marsh said. 'But I'm not married so I can't really say which one I'd go for.'

'Well, I'm married and I might go mad at my wife but I wouldn't kill her. Unless my temper became uncontrollable.'

'So why would Doctor Wilson kill Sir Reginald?'

'Perhaps he'd been after Sara Wilson for some time. She's an attractive woman, early forties. Sir Reginald might have had sex with her in the past, but this time the doctor decided to put an end to it, once and for all,' said Bill.

'Could be,' Marsh agreed. 'Well, whatever happened, we'll need to have a friendly chat with Mrs Wilson. And we can see if she gets uncomfortable when we tell her we've heard Sir Reginald was having an affair just before he was murdered.'

'But before we do that, Sergeant, let's go and see Robson.'

The meeting with Paul Robson had seemed a waste of time. Apart from establishing that he had hidden in the single room for the murder game, he was unable to be more specific regarding who else was in the room at the time. His wife was only able to repeat what she had told them on Saturday night and couldn't be sure who the other people in the main bedroom were.

It was as they were leaving that Paul Robson beckoned them into his office, closing the door behind them.

Keeping his voice low, Paul said, 'I didn't want Sheila to hear, but I heard something this morning that might or might not be true about Sara Wilson and Reggie.'

'And what was that?' Bill asked.

'Well, Ken Morris was at a golf club dinner in Dorking, in Surrey, last night, and heard that Sara had been having a ding-dong with Reggie at the hotel there. Apparently they used the place on two or three occasions.'

Bill and Marsh exchanged glances and Bill said, 'By a ding-dong, I take it you mean having sex.'

'Yes. Ken said the maitre d' at the hotel in Dorking said the room was booked for the night, but she only came for an hour or so during the afternoon. Then at night he had a different woman there. Well, that's what he told Ken.'

'When he said "a different woman", did he mean the same woman or different women?'

'No idea. You'll have to ask Ken if *he* knows. Like I said, my wife doesn't know and Ken didn't tell Angie either. The girls couldn't keep it to themselves for long. You know what they're like when they get their teeth into a bit of scandal. But Ken and I thought you should know.'

'Thank you, Mr Robson.'

After they left, Inspector Forward and Sergeant Marsh made contact with Ken Morris at his office. He confirmed the story Paul Robson had told them but was unable to say who it was that stayed with Sir Reginald at night on those occasions. When they got back to the office, Bill telephoned the maitre d' at the White Hart hotel in Dorking, who told him that the girl was the same one each time, and that she was very attractive, about twenty with blonde hair. But he didn't know what her name was because the man always addressed her as 'love'. He also thought the man was paying for the girl's favours by the way they behaved. He didn't think the girl was local as he had not seen her before. Bill thanked him and hung up.

'What did he say?' asked Marsh.

'The girl was a young blonde. Same one each time and could be on the game according to him. But he didn't think she was a local.'

'Well, if he was having sex with Sara Wilson in the afternoon, and then a young blonde at night, the old boy must have had stamina. But on the other hand, he might not have been seeing the doctor's wife to have sex. He might have needed to meet her for a completely different reason.'

'That thought had crossed my mind,' said Bill. 'But *what* reason? If it wasn't for sex why did they have to meet in a hotel out at Dorking? What the hell were they up to?'

CHAPTER TWELVE

Father O'Connor had been visiting his friend Father Brady in Greenwich, south London. They had studied in Rome together as young students and not met up for some time. After having had a pleasant morning with his old friend, he was on his way to see Terry Kennedy when he had to stop at traffic lights. As he waited for the lights to turn green, Father O'Connor caught sight of a man he thought was Tony Farrow come out of a newsagents in a side street. He watched as the man got into a car and drive away. He sat wondering what Farrow would be doing in south London, when he understood from Inspector Forward that he was in Wales. He realized it could have been a coincidence that the man looked like Farrow, but wanted to remember the car's registration number, just in case. He was hurriedly looking for a pencil to write it down with when the lights turned to green and cars behind started blowing their horns. He gave an apologetic wave and drove away, hoping he would remember most of the number.

Fiona was sitting at her dressing table in the bedroom thinking of Edward. She couldn't believe the way their love-making last night had been so special to her. Although she was aware of the need to be discreet, she wanted to get her husband's funeral over and done with so that she could get on with her life again, without having to hide from gossiping friends. When the phone rang she quickly answered it.

'Hello.'

'This is John Brett, solicitor, your ladyship.'

Fiona was disappointed the call was from the solicitor's office and not Edward. 'Yes, Mr Brett.'

'I am sorry to disturb you at this difficult time, but I do need to know whether your late husband made a more recent will to the one he made last year.'

Fiona was confused by his question and hesitated before answering. 'I'm sorry. Your question came as a surprise to me. Are you saying he made a new will last year?'

'Yes.'

'I had no idea he had done so.'

'Oh, I see.'

'Why did he want to do that? I mean, what changes did he make from the earlier one?'

'I'm afraid that with a murder enquiry taking place I cannot divulge the contents at this time, m'lady.'

'I don't understand,' Fiona said. 'You tell me that Reggie made a new will last year and ask if he made a more recent one. Surely, as his solicitor, you would know if he made a more recent one?'

'It's just that he was very secretive at times and I wanted to make sure he hadn't made another will with someone else. You see my predicament if he had.'

Fiona was worried as she asked, 'Does the new will change *my* position in any way?'

'I'm sure you will find he made generous provision for you, m'lady.'

She was now becoming curious and asked, 'Who was it that told you about my husband's death?'

There was the sound of papers being handled when he replied, 'We received a letter from a Philippa Pane.'

Fiona was getting suspicious. 'My husband didn't die until Saturday, so she must have posted it on Sunday, before she herself died. I wonder how she knew your name and address?'

Instead of an answer she heard a click and the dialling tone. Her reaction was to call the solicitor herself and check as to whether Mr Brett had actually telephoned her. But first she thought she would have a look in the security box where Reggie kept his private documents. It would mean going into his study for the first time since seeing him dead, and the thought of it brought a cold shudder down her spine, as it did before. This made her decide to ask Mrs Romaine to bring the box to the sitting room for her.

The key to the security box was on the ring with Reggie's car keys. When she opened the box, there were only two envelopes and they were sealed. One was marked 'birth and marriage certificates' and the other was marked 'house deeds etc'. But there was nothing else except his passport, US dollars, some Euros and recent property purchasing documents. Fiona had no idea where a copy of his will could be and gave up the intention to search for it. Instead, she decided to call Mr Brett. She found his number in the phone book and dialled. The voice that answered was not that of the person she had been talking to.

'John Brett,' he said.

'This is Lady Pace-Warren.'

'Good morning, ma'am.'

'I am sorry to bother you, Mr Brett, but I wonder if you could tell me. Did my husband make a new will last year?'

'No, m'lady. The last will was made when you married. Is there a particular reason for your asking?'

'Well, yes. My husband was killed on Saturday evening.

And I wondered if there was a will *other* than the one you refer to.'

'No, no. Killed, you say. May I offer my sincere condolences.'

'Thank you.'

'Was it a road accident?'

'No. He was murdered.' As she said it she was surprised at the lack of sadness in her voice and quickly added with some feeling, 'It was such a terrible shock.'

'I am completely stunned by the news. It was only a few days ago that Sir Reginald phoned to ask me the legal position on a business venture he was considering. Well, I really am shocked to hear your news.'

'Thank you,' Fiona said in a tone of sincerity. 'And thank you for confirming that nothing has changed from his original wishes.'

'Oh, no,' said Mr Brett. 'You have nothing to worry about there.'

'Well, thank you for putting my mind at rest. Goodbye.'

'Goodbye, m'lady.'

Fiona hung up, and then decided to call Inspector Forward to see if there was still any restriction on her arranging the funeral. She found the card he had left her and dialled the number. It was answered by Sergeant Cooper at the front desk, who told her Inspector Forward and Sergeant Marsh were out but available on their mobile phones. Fiona decided not to bother the inspector until he was back in his office.

Bill Forward telephoned Sara Wilson with the intention of making an appointment to ask her a few questions. But when he learned that she was alone at the moment and that her husband was visiting at the hospital, he and Marsh lost no time in seeing her. After the usual pleasantries, he went briefly over her statement of Saturday, as if checking that he and Marsh had her movements correctly recorded. He waited until she seemed relaxed and then asked, 'Did you ever hear anyone say that Sir Reginald might be having an affair with a woman in Dorking, Mrs Wilson?'

Her reaction was just what he was hoping for. She tried to conceal her surprise at the unexpected question and forced an innocent smile of interest. 'And did they say who the woman was?'

'She was seen on more than one occasion,' said Marsh. 'Once in a car park, and at least twice leaving the White Hart hotel.'

'Apparently he would meet her first and then have a young blonde spend the night with him,' Bill said.

Sara Wilson knew there was no point in pretending any more and said, 'You obviously know that it was me somebody saw leave the hotel. But I had no idea he had a young blonde go there for the night. What a bastard. Can I ask who it was that saw me there?'

'Philippa Pane,' said Bill. 'She kept a day-to-day record of everything in her diary. Now I'd like to ask you what you were doing there. And remember, this is a murder investigation that I'm holding, Mrs Wilson. I'm not interested in your personal life but if you *were* having an affair I would like to know *why* you were. In your statement on Saturday you said …' He looked at Marsh to quote her.

The sergeant read from his notebook. '"Fiona's girlfriends, including myself, often wondered if Reggie had a bit on the side. But we had no proof. No proof at all."'

'Do you remember saying that?' asked Bill.

She became embarrassed as she said, 'Yes, I do. But I'm not a bit that he had on the side, I assure you. Oh, he tried it on, as he did with most women. But he didn't get very far with me. He only tried it once and that was in his car at Dorking.

The randy bugger pulled my skirt up but when I threatened to tell David, he let go and pretended he was only joking. That was the one and only time, Inspector.'

'So will you tell me why you met Sir Reginald at that hotel?'

Sara was obviously reluctant to tell him. 'Is it possible that what I'm about to tell you can remain private, at least for the time being? I don't think Fiona could take it after what she's going through at the moment. I know she's got the police-woman there but the shock of what I'm going to tell you would knock her for six.'

'We shall not mention anything unless we have to. You have my word on that. Now, can you tell me why you were secretly meeting Sir Reginald in Dorking.'

'During a dinner party at Fiona's, we were talking and I happened to mention that I had once worked in the records department of Social Services. It was about eight weeks ago that Reggie called me and asked to meet me in private to discuss a very personal matter. It had to be somewhere away from London and because he had a business meeting in Dorking, suggested that we met there. Naturally, I was intrigued and agreed. Anyway, we met at the White Hart hotel where he had his meeting arranged. He told me that he'd had an affair many years ago and that the woman had become pregnant and that he'd paid for her to have an abortion. He had believed that was the end of the matter until he received a phone call from a man, claiming to be his son. The man said he had been brought up in a foster home but that his natural mother had traced him and told him she was terminally ill and that Reggie was his father. Apparently the woman had decided to keep the money Reggie had given her for the abortion and have the child. Naturally this came as a hell of a shock to him. The reason he wanted to meet me was to ask my advice as to what he could do. But when he parked the car at the hotel I knew he had more than advice on his mind. That's when he tried to get his hand under my skirt. And that must have been when Philippa saw us. But that was the only time he did it.'

'Even so, despite that incident, you still went back to the hotel with him on at least two other occasions. You apparently went willingly into the bedroom with him each time. But why? Surely that was asking for trouble.'

Sara became uncomfortable again. 'I wanted to find out who the man was that claimed he was Reggie's son. And tried to think of the best way for Reggie to check up on him and see if he really *was* his son. Otherwise he was leaving himself wide open for blackmail. And he knew that if this got out his reputation as an astute businessman would be ruined.'

'Couldn't you have done that without going to Dorking, Mrs Wilson?' Marsh asked her.

'Why couldn't Sir Reginald demand this man had a DNA? Or hire a private detective?' asked Bill.

Sara became emotional as she replied, 'I had to go to the hotel with him. He threatened to tell David I'd been if I didn't.'

'So you *did* have sex with him,' said Bill.

Reluctantly she said, 'Yes. I had to. Otherwise my marriage would have been in jeopardy. You don't know what he was like, Inspector.'

'I only know that he's dead, Mrs Wilson. And that someone there at the party on Saturday killed him. Now, apart from yourself, who do you think had a reason for killing him?'

There was a sudden look of shocked disbelief on her face at his question. 'For God's sake, Inspector, you don't think *I* killed him!'

'You were being forced to have sex with a man you say was threatening to tell your husband you were with him at the hotel if you didn't. That gave you a motive for killing him, didn't it?'

'I told you the truth, for God's sake. I didn't kill Reggie. He wasn't raping me! I did what he wanted in order to protect my marriage, and that's the truth. If David ever found out, he would leave me and I couldn't bear that. And Fiona would never forgive me.'

'But sooner or later, she's bound to find out he had a son. Then what will you do? Pretend you didn't know?' asked Marsh.

'Sergeant Marsh has a point there,' Bill said. 'Did you ever actually find out anything about this young man? Or was it just an excuse Sir Reginald made up in order to get you into bed with him?'

'No. There *was* a son. But where he went when he left his home I wasn't able to find out. But the boy does exist. Reggie said he telephoned on two or three occasions recently and made threats to kill him if he didn't make arrangements for large amounts of money to be paid to him.'

Marsh asked, 'Did he say when the most recent of these calls were made? I ask because his wife overheard what she thought was a threatening phone call within the past two weeks.'

'He told me the boy had phoned just over a week, ago.' Sara said.

'When did he tell you this?' asked Bill.

'He phoned me just before he went up north last week. That was the last time I spoke to him. I didn't even see him on Saturday. It's bizarre, isn't it? One minute he was in his study and the next thing I knew David was telling us he was dead.'

'What was the boy's name?' asked Marsh.

'His foster parents christened him Anthony. He was a nice friendly lad, according to the Farrows. But once he discovered who his father was he started to get nasty and began threatening him for money.'

'And his natural mother is now dead?' said Bill.

'Yes, she died a while ago,' Sara replied, then quickly said, 'You won't have to tell Fiona about Reggie and me, will you? Please don't. It was just a stupid thing that I did and I don't want to hurt her. I just hope she never finds out about him having a son.'

'If he contacts her for money she will soon know he exists,' Bill told her. Then after a few moments, he said, 'We shall go now, Mrs Wilson. But you will remain a suspect until I am certain the information you have given us is the truth. I would like you to give me the name of the person I should talk to at Social Services.'

Sara became very nervous. 'It would be easier if I made any enquiries on your behalf. I've worked there and I know the best contacts. Whereas an official police enquiry could make them suspicious and prevent them giving you the confidential information you want.'

'That's very kind of you. But I would like the name of the person to contact. My superintendent will expect to see it on my report sheet, you understand. But I will call you if I need your help in contacting them, Mrs Wilson.'

Sara felt slightly relieved as she said, 'It's Marjorie Calder you need to talk to.'

Bill thanked her and he and Marsh left. As they got into the car and drove off, Marsh said, 'What do you think about Tony Farrow being the prodigal son? Do you believe her?'

Bill sat back in the passenger seat. 'I'll tell you what I think, sunshine. I think there's more to this than she's admitting to. We might have a better idea when we've phoned Social Services and enquired about the adopted boy.' He suddenly flinched as they passed a line of traffic. 'Drive carefully, please. You don't have a flashing blue light on this car, remember.'

Back in his office, Inspector Forward phoned Father O'Connor to see if he had any news on Terry Kennedy. After telling him that Terry would be released by the weekend, he told him of his journey back from visiting his friend in south London.

'I wondered if you were sure that Tony Farrow was in Wales. Only I thought I saw him, or his double, when I was driving home through south London this morning.'

'He was in Cardiff when I telephoned him,' Bill said. 'He answered the phone himself. So it must have been someone who looked like him. If you're seeing things you either blessed too much wine with your friend, or you need your eyes tested and shouldn't be driving a car,' Bill said jokingly. 'It's good news about Terry, though. I shall try and get over to see him today. I would have been earlier but I've got a lot on my plate at the moment.' Marsh signalled him to pick up the extension phone. 'Sorry, Father, I've got to go. My sergeant's telling me I'm wanted.' He picked up the other phone and said, 'Inspector Forward.'

'It's Sergeant Cooper, sir. There was a call for you earlier from a lady who wanted to speak to you and I think it's her again, Lady Pace-Warren.'

'Put her through.' He waited till she'd been connected and said, 'Inspector Forward, your ladyship. What can I do for you?'

'I received a call from a man claiming to be our solicitor. He asked me if there was a will later than the one my husband made last year. I became confused because I thought the only will was the one that was drawn up when we married. Anyway, I became suspicious when he appeared to get fidgety and rang off very quickly. I phoned our solicitor myself but he knew nothing of the phone call or another will. It's obvious that the first caller was not our solicitor but someone searching for information. I thought I should tell you.'

'You did right, ma'am. And you have no idea who this man might have been?'

'None, but he obviously knew Reggie was dead. And I should have known it wasn't the solicitor because his voice was too young for it to be Mr Brett.'

'If the young man rings again, can you record the call and let me know immediately, please?'

'I've never tried the recording facility because my husband used it on automatic for all his business calls. But I'm sure I could manage it.'

'Kate Weston will check it for you. And get her to see if any of the calls he received are still on there. Just in case the man you think was threatening him made a more recent call.'

'Yes. I'll do that, Inspector.'

'Thank you, ma'am.' He hung up and looked across at Marsh, who had been listening to the call. 'Well, Sergeant, it looks as if Farrow is going to be a problem for her. It'll be interesting to see if he shows up to contest the will if Sir Reginald hasn't made him a recipient. Ring the Social Services and see what they can tell you about this boy and find out if either of his parents are on their records. And if they don't want to be co-operative threaten them with a search warrant and make sure they know it's a murder enquiry. You know the drill. I'm going to pop over and see the Kennedy lad. I won't be long.'

As soon as Bill went out of the office, Marsh looked up the phone number of the Social Services. He dialled the number and heard a recorded message.

'This is the Social Services. I'm afraid we cannot answer your call at the moment. Please leave your name and number with a brief message and we'll get back to you as soon as possible. If your call is of an urgent nature please call Mrs Anderson on her mobile. The number is ...'

Marsh hung up and decided to try again later. He was about to get on with his paperwork when his mobile phone rang and he answered it. 'DS Marsh.'

'My name is Robert Conway. I had a voicemail asking me to call this number.'

'Oh yes. I wonder if you can tell me, sir, did Philippa Pane have any relatives that you know of?'

'She had a sister, I think. But she died in Australia I believe. I don't think there was anyone else. Not that I know of anyway. Why do you ask?'

'Miss Pane was killed in her apartment and we are trying to notify any relatives she might have.'

'Philippa dead! Good God.'

'I'm sorry to be the bearer of bad news, sir, but you were the only person we knew that she was friendly with.'

'How was she killed? It wasn't an electric shock from her old kettle, was it? I warned her about that bare lead. It was so dangerous.'

'It wasn't the kettle, sir. Someone beat her over the head.'

There was a silence before Robert Conway spoke. 'I cannot believe it. She wanted me to go to a party with her on Saturday but I couldn't go. Oh, poor woman. What will happen now?'

'We will wait for the post mortem and the inquest. Once the coroner is satisfied, her funeral can take place.'

'Unless another relative can be found, I shall make the funeral arrangements. Please keep me informed.' His voice was sounding stressed as he ended the call.

CHAPTER THIRTEEN

Fiona was still reluctant to go into the study, so Kate Weston took the telephone into the dining room and connected it to the phone socket. They sat next to each other while they listened to just five recorded messages. They were all business conversations but not one that Fiona could recognize as the voice of the man she had heard threatening her husband.

'That's the end of them,' said Kate. 'I won't delete them, just in case we need any of them later. I'll put this back in the study for now.' She disconnected the phone, took it back to the study and put it on the desk. As she turned to leave she saw that Fiona had followed her and was standing nervously at the door.

'I know it's silly, but I haven't even been this close to the study until now,' Fiona said. 'I can still see him there.'

'I can understand that,' said Kate, 'but there's nothing here to hurt you. It's a bit like falling off a bicycle or a horse. You have to get back on as soon as you can or you never will.'

Fiona knew Kate was right but stood there hesitating before walking into the room. She went in, trying not to look at the desk but found it impossible to avoid. She stood in front of it for a moment, facing the fireplace, then turned around and looked across the desk to the window. She took a deep breath and said with relief, 'I did it, Kate. I came in.'

'It wasn't so difficult, was it? All you needed was somebody here with you.'

'Thanks, Kate. Now let's get out of here and have a cup of tea. I'll see if Mrs Romaine's in the kitchen, then we can go and have a chat. I'd like to know more about you. If you don't mind, that is.'

'No, of course I don't mind,' said Kate, wondering what Fiona wanted to know about her.

Mrs Romaine was making some rock cakes when Fiona walked into the kitchen.

'Could we have a pot of tea, please?'

'Would you like it in the living room?' Mrs Romaine asked.

'Yes, please. It's comfortable in there. I see you're making some of your delicious rock cakes.'

'Yes, m'lady. But they won't be ready for a while.'

'That's all right,' said Fiona. 'I don't mind waiting. Your cakes are always worth waiting for.'

Always enjoying a compliment, Mrs Romaine smiled, 'Thank you, m'lady.'

Fiona went back to the living room and saw Kate looking at the photographs on the writing desk.

'Before you ask me what you wanted to, do you mind if I ask *you* a personal question?' asked Kate.

'Fire away,' said Fiona.

'I've noticed that there are no photographs of your husband anywhere. Not on his own or with you. Why is that? Was he camera shy?'

'He hated anyone pointing a camera at him. Ever since I first knew him he was the same. The only photographs were of our wedding and he only liked the ones of me alone or with my maid of honour or friends. He got rid of any with him in except for the usual one of the bride and groom. He kept that on his desk for quite a while. One day I asked him why it wasn't there any more and he said, "Because I don't look like that any more and I don't want reminding of it." There was an older one of him on his own but that seemed to vanish, so he must have hidden it or got rid of it. I've never seen it since.'

Kate screwed up her face and said, 'How very odd.'

'He could be strange at times. But he looked after me more than most men look after their wives. I never wanted for anything at first. Then after a while he changed and became jealous and possessive. He even began to begrudge my having friends round. And yet I could still have whatever I wanted.'

'Except love and affection. If you'd had that you wouldn't have wanted Mr King to come and stay the night with you.'

Fiona gave a sigh, and with a nod of agreement said, 'I know. Life can be very unfair sometimes. Now tell me about you. I don't really know anything about the police officer who's living here with me.'

'What do you want to know?' asked Kate.

Fiona wanted to know everything about her, but began by asking, 'Do you often have to leave home, and your family, to be a bodyguard to someone like me?'

'I live alone. So I don't have to leave a husband or children, if that's what you're wondering. And my parents understand that my job often means my working a lot away from home. They know I like my job. And although I'm sure they would prefer me to live at home with them, they realize it's more practical to be in a place of my own. What else would you like to know?'

'What about a boyfriend?' asked Fiona.

'There's a chap at the station that I've been out with a few times. But it's nothing serious at the moment.'

Mrs Romaine came in with a pot of tea on the tray and said, 'The rock cakes won't be ready for another twenty minutes, so I thought you might like some biscuits.'

Fiona was disappointed that there were no rock cakes but the plate of assorted biscuits proved too tempting for her and Kate to ignore. They were about to enjoy the tea when the telephone rang. Fiona answered it, hoping it was Edward, but it was David Wilson.

'Hello, Fiona. How are you feeling today? Have you taken the capsules I gave you?'

'I'm feeling fine, thank you, David. And yes, I have taken the capsules you gave me.'

'I want to come round and check your blood pressure. I have to check it before you take another capsule. Just to make sure everything is going as it should. I'll see you in a few minutes then,' he said and hung up.

'That was Doctor Wilson. He's coming round soon to take my blood pressure. Sorry about that. Never mind. The good thing is the rock cakes will be ready by the time he goes,' she said with a grin.

Inspector Forward was in a good mood when he got back from seeing Terry Kennedy. He walked into the office and told Marsh how pleased he was with Terry's progress.

'He's looking more like his old self again. Amazing how much he's improved since I last saw him. I must say they've really looked after him in that hospital. They're letting him out in a couple of days, sunshine.'

'I'm glad to hear it, sir. Surprising what rest and the right medicine will do,' said Marsh.

'How did you get on with the Social Services?'

'They were on an answerphone when I rang. I didn't bother to leave a message. I thought I'd wait till you got back and see what you wanted to do.'

'Don't worry, call them again. There must be somebody there.'

CHAPTER FOURTEEN

The Robertson Orphanage was an old imposing building, built during the Victorian era, but reminiscent of something from *Oliver Twist*. The first sight of it from the old iron gates was not one of a place to put children in. Although it had been closed for several years, he could see through the large split in the oak door that it had at one time boasted a large hall leading to a massive oak staircase. Although it was now crumbling, they gave it the appearance of an old mansion that may have once belonged to a family of opulence. Tony Farrow stood looking at it and wondered how many children had been forced to live in these places in past years. And he wondered why it had been allowed to stay there in decay for so long. He was suddenly grateful to Robert and Patricia Farrow for taking him into their home when he had been abandoned by his mother. The same mother who had used the internet to check on the Social Services babies that had been left there on the day he was taken in by them. There had only been the one and she had contacted him before her death. As he walked away from the building, he began to think of the woman who had brought him into the world and wondered what his life would have been like if she had lived. And now he had a father that he despised and

Tony Farrow intended to make him pay for what he had done.

Fiona was starting to feel like a prisoner in her own home and told Kate so.

'I really wish your inspector would let me go out.'

'I'm afraid you can't just yet. Sorry.'

'It's just that I want to get some fresh air in my lungs and go to the shops. It seems ages since I last went out of the house.'

'I know. But you must try and be patient a bit longer.'

'I keep thinking how nice it would be if I could go out with Edward to a restaurant or call in at our local pub for a drink like normal people do.'

'You will soon.'

'Yes but how soon? That's what I want to know.' A smile came as she said, 'I remember once getting really drunk on cider.'

'When was this?'

'On my seventeenth birthday. I had been introduced to cider by a boy who rather fancied me.'

'Not Edward!'

Fiona laughed. 'No. This was a boy who thought he was God's gift. Anyway, I had never drunk cider before and at first I didn't think it was that wonderful. Anyway, the boy made me have another one and then another. Suddenly everything went round and round and I nearly fell over.'

'So what happened?'

'Well, the next thing I knew was Norman, that was his name, was trying to get me into the bedroom.'

'Whose house were you in?' asked Kate, smiling.

'Norman's. His parents were away so he thought he was on to a good thing.'

'So what happened?'

'We were halfway up the stairs when I realized what he was doing and what his intentions were. I pushed him away from me and he fell down the stairs and banged his head.'

'Was he hurt?'

'His pride was. Two of the boys got him into the bedroom and he laid on the bed nursing a sore head. I sat with one of the girls drinking coffee until I was fit enough to go home.'

Kate chuckled. 'Well, Norman got his wish and ended up on the bed.'

'Yes but not with me,' laughed Fiona.

'What happened to him?'

'The last I heard was that he married and went to live in Africa somewhere. Have you ever been really drunk, Kate?'

'Police officers never get drunk,' She replied with a grin.

Fiona smiled. 'I shall miss you when this is all over and you have to go. It would be nice if we could remain friends.' The front doorbell rang. 'That will be David coming to check my blood pressure.'

Sara Wilson was wondering if she had done the right thing by telling the police about her sexual liaisons with Reggie. It was the fear of David ever finding out that really worried her. The thought of him leaving her was nagging at her subconscious and she couldn't imagine what she would do if she was left alone at her age. She looked at her watch and as she began to think she had made a mistake with the time she had agreed to meet Angie and Sheila, she saw them hurrying towards her.

'Hello, Sara,' Sheila said. 'Have you been waiting long?'

'No. I've only just arrived myself.'

'Where shall we go? Do you girls fancy some tea and a light snack?' said Sheila.

'I really don't mind,' said Angie.

'What about the little place round the corner?' suggested Sara. 'It's cosy in there.'

'Good idea,' said Angie, as they walked to the cafeteria. Once they were settled at a table, Angie asked Sara, 'How's David?'

'Busy as usual. He's going to see Fiona after surgery to give her a check-up.'

'As long as that's *all* he gives her,' Angie said with a saucy wink.

'Don't be naughty. She's got that Edward for anything she might need in that department,' said Sara.

'Seriously, though, you must ask David if that Edward is ever around when he goes there,' said Angie. 'I bet he is. He'll be hiding in the bedroom until David's gone, then she'll rush up and let him ravish her.'

They laughed and then the waitress arrived to take their order. The rest of their time was taken up discussing Fiona, the policewoman, Philippa, and their husbands, Ken and Paul, with Sara pretending to enjoy their scandalous chat but constantly wondering what they would be saying about her if they knew what had gone on at the hotel in Dorking.

Doctor Wilson had finished checking Fiona's blood pressure and was happy with the result. Kate had left them alone in the sitting room and David was pleased to have Fiona to himself while he talked privately to her.

'Although your blood pressure doesn't give me cause for concern, I'm not happy about you staying in this house. I know you have Mrs Romaine here whenever you want her, but being here where Reggie was murdered is not right. As your doctor, I know that you could be heading for a delayed reaction to what has happened and that does concern me.

You shouldn't be alone at night. Sara agrees with me.'

'I've got Kate with me, David. And she's nice. We get on really well together.'

'She's a policewoman, Fiona. Not a friend like Sara and me. We'd like you to come and stay with us. It would make us feel better.'

'I promise you I'm fine, really,' Fiona insisted. 'But thank you for the offer. I really do appreciate it.'

'Well, you know where we are if you change your mind.'

He got up from his seat and Fiona walked to the door with him. After he'd gone, Kate came from the kitchen, smiling.

'The rock cakes are out of the oven and cooling down. They smell delicious,' she said. 'What did the doctor say?'

'My blood pressure is OK but he's worried about me being here in this house. I might be heading for some sort of breakdown he thinks. So he wants me to go and stay with him and his wife. He doesn't know that Edward stayed with me last night, of course.'

'Have you heard from him today?'

'No. I don't know why he hasn't phoned. I expected to hear from him before now. It's funny how I miss him. Do you think I'm just being silly?'

'Perhaps he's got tied up somewhere.'

Fiona gave her a cheeky look as she said, 'I don't think he's into that sort of thing. At least I hope not.' Before she could say anything else, the telephone rang. 'Excuse me,' she said and answered the call. She was delighted to hear Edward's voice.

'Hello, gorgeous. Sorry I didn't call you earlier but I had a problem.'

She sounded anxious as she asked, 'What happened?'

'My mobile wasn't charged so I couldn't use the darn thing.'

'Oh, is that all?' she said with relief. Then she told Kate

who it was. 'It's Edward. I'm just telling Kate who it is. We've been sitting here chatting.'

Kate indicated that she would leave Fiona to talk in private and went into the hall, closing the door behind her.

'Say hello to her for me,' said Edward. 'I normally put the phone in the charger when I go to bed. But last night I forgot to take the charger with me.' His voice was a sexy whisper as he said, 'I had other things on my mind when I came to you last night. Though I can't think why, can you?'

Fiona wished she could see him and wanted him close to her again as she said, 'I wish this was last night.'

'So do I.'

'Can't you come round? Then you can tell me what you've been doing today. There's only Kate and Mrs Romaine here.'

'I really do want to see you and tell you my news. But what if someone should see me?'

'If anyone should call here, you could always hide until I get rid of them. We managed to keep you out of sight yesterday. Please come. I need you here with me. Please.'

There was a moment of silence and then he said, 'If I *am* seen, your reputation will be ruined and you'll have to move right away from the area. You know that.'

'I want to move anyway as soon as this awful mess has been sorted out with the police investigation, and the funeral is over.'

She thought she could hear a smile in his voice as he said, 'You've talked me into it. I'll be there as soon as I can.'

The fact that he was coming made her feel happy again and she went to tell Kate and Mrs Romaine that he was on his way. After she had told them, she decided it was time to go and check herself in the spare bedroom mirror. When she sat at the dressing table she could see the reflection of the bed where she and Edward had made love the previous night. She closed her eyes and imagined them together again tonight.

CHAPTER FIFTEEN

Robert Conway was trying to come to terms with Philippa's death. He found it hard to believe she had been murdered. The way their relationship had developed was something he had enjoyed from the time they first met a few years earlier. He was remembering the way they had gone to her apartment and had an evening of frantic sexual activity. And the way he had introduced her to the use of sexual aids that he had purchased from a Soho sex shop. And now she was dead and their uninhibited times together were suddenly ended. He was now grateful for the new relationship he had found with a widow he had befriended, and was certain that with patience he could cultivate her in the same way he had Philippa.

It was with these thoughts going through his mind that he suddenly remembered a name. It was the name of a woman that Philippa had said was her cousin. The name that he remembered was Celia Benton, and Philippa had said she lived somewhere in Kent. He knew that if the police could trace her it would remove any problems of funeral arrangements from his shoulders and he decided to phone Chelsea police station. He couldn't remember the name of the policeman he had spoken to, so he asked for the man in charge of Philippa Pane's murder investigation.

*

Fiona was still in the bedroom when the front doorbell rang. She knew that Edward couldn't have got there so quickly and hoped that whoever it was could be got rid of before he arrived. She stood at the top of the stairs and watched as Mrs Romaine went to the door. A tall man was standing there. He was in his thirties and spoke with an air of over-confidence.

'Good afternoon. I'd like to speak to Lady Pace-Warren. May I come in?'

As he made a move to enter the hall, Mrs Romaine blocked his way and stood firmly in position. 'Who are you? Do you have an appointment?'

'I'm from the *Gazette*. I believe Sir Reginald was murdered here on Saturday night. Can you confirm that?'

'May I ask where you got that information from?' she said.

He answered her with a smirk. 'We have our ways. Now, may I speak with her ladyship? I would do a nice sympathetic piece before the nationals get wind of it. If you know what I mean.'

'Perhaps you would be kind enough to give me your card and I will see if her ladyship is at home,' said Mrs Romaine with a false smile.

'That's more like it.' He took a business card from his pocket and gave it to her. 'If you're the housekeeper, I can do a nice piece on you as well. I believe you're the one who found him. That must have been a nasty shock.'

She took his card and closed the door, leaving him standing on the doorstep. As she stepped back into the hall, Kate came to her from the living room where she had been listening. Fiona came downstairs and joined them.

'I don't like the sound of it,' Kate said. 'He could be trouble.'

'I agree,' said Mrs Romaine. 'I only had to look at him to see that he's a nasty bit of work.'

'We've got to get rid of him before Edward arrives or God knows what he might write,' Fiona said anxiously.

'What's this reporter's name? I'll give Inspector Forward a call and see what he wants us to do,' said Kate.

'Simon Korer,' said Mrs Romaine, reading his card.

Kate used her mobile and got through to Bill Forward.

'It's PC Weston, sir. We've got a Simon Korer at the front door. He's from the local gazette and wants to interview her ladyship. He knows about the murder and the fact that it was Mrs Romaine who found Sir Reginald. We can't stall him much longer so what do you want us to do?'

'Tell him she's resting and not well enough to talk to the press at the moment. Suggest he comes back in the morning. Has he seen you yet?' asked Bill.

'No, sir.'

'Good. Keep out of sight until he's gone. I'll come over later.'

'Right sir, Edward King is on his way too.'

'Christ! If the press see him there *will* be trouble. Get rid of the reporter and keep your fingers crossed he's out of the way before King turns up. Get her ladyship to ring him on his mobile and warn him. I'll see you as soon as I can.'

Kate relayed her inspector's instructions to the others and went with Fiona to the living room. While she tried to contact Edward, Mrs Romaine went to the door and composed herself before opening it.

'I am sorry to keep you, Mr Korer. I'm afraid her ladyship is not well enough to see you at the moment. But she asked if you could come back in the morning.' Then she added with a smile, 'I'm sure she'll be feeling better by then.'

'Right. I'll see you in the morning then. Eleven o'clock? I'll only be with her for half an hour. Then I'll get my copy in to make our deadline and beat the nationals to the story. I want mine to be an exclusive. Then I can join the big boys and make real money.'

'I'm sure you'll be successful. Goodbye for now, Mr Korer.' Closing the door she went to the cloakroom window and watched him get into his car and drive away. Satisfied, she went to tell Kate and Fiona. 'It's all right. He's gone.'

'Are you sure, or is he just hanging about outside to see who comes and goes?' asked Fiona.

'The way he drove off I don't think he was in the mood to wait around outside,' Mrs Romaine answered. 'He wasn't too happy about waiting until tomorrow for his interview.'

'I'm sure the inspector will come up with something when he gets here, so don't worry,' said Kate.

'The press are beginning to get word of Sir Reginald's death so I'm going over to see her ladyship,' Bill Forward told Marsh. 'And King is on his way there too. I just hope a news-hungry lad with a camera doesn't start taking pictures and stirring things up. I'm going to get a quick cup of coffee. While I'm gone, see if you can get our Kent boys to find this Celia Benton woman and give you her phone number.'

'Shall I ring her and tell her about Philippa Pane?' asked Marsh. 'Or do you want them to do it?'

'I don't mind. As long as somebody tells her and arranges the funeral. We should have the post mortem result in soon and then, hopefully, the coroner will call an opening inquest and issue certificates for both funerals to go ahead.'

While the inspector went to the canteen, Marsh got on to the Kent constabulary.

Bill sat drinking his coffee and thinking about the case he was investigating. He felt sure there was something he was missing and that annoyed him. He wanted to make an arrest and get the case wrapped up. In his mind he was convinced that the killer of Sir Reginald Pace-Warren and Philippa Pane was the same person but he had no proof of this. If only Mr Neville had seen the person leave Philippa Pane's apartment and hurry down the stairs. Then he would know whether her killer was a man or a woman. Bill thought his frustration was making him lose sight of some evidence that should be staring him in the face. He wondered if someone at the party on Saturday night had deliberately lied to him in order to avoid him learning the truth about who they were with, and what they were really doing at the time of the murder. He finished his coffee and went back to his office.

'Are you sure you won't want me there with you, sir? After all, you'll be alone there with three women. You might need some protection.' Marsh grinned.

'You could be right, Marsh. You could take care of the lovely housekeeper while I get ravished by the other two.'

Marsh cringed as he said, 'The housekeeper! I've just remembered I've got some paperwork to do. Have a good time, sir. And don't forget you'll have Edward King there if you need any help.'

Bill Forward ignored Marsh's remark and took Tony Farrow's photograph from the drawer and put it in his pocket. 'I know it's a shot in the dark but I'll let the housekeeper see if she recognizes Farrow's face.'

Marsh looked puzzled as he asked, 'Why would she have seen him?'

'I'm still interested in the meter reader and you never know. It might have been Farrow. I can only ask. After all, he must have had a reason to be on our patch, other than to have sex with Mandy Lucas. Assuming that is what he was with her for and not something more devious. Anyway it's worth a try.'

*

After being held up in the heavy traffic, Edward King's taxi pulled into the drive of Stafford House so as to conceal the identity of the occupant from the prying eyes of any nosy neighbour. Although he was looking forward to telling Fiona his news, he was worried that she might not want to stay in the area after what had happened. And it was the thought of that possibility that was bothering him. He knew that all his hopes relied on her willingness to remain in a reasonable distance of Chelsea and Fulham.

He paid the taxi and as he picked up his briefcase, he saw the front door of the house open and Fiona standing there with a big welcoming smile. He hurried to her and went into the hall, where he took her in his arms and kissed her.

'Oh, I've missed you today,' Fiona told him. 'You don't know how much.'

He looked around and asked quietly, 'Where are the others?'

'Mrs Romaine is in the kitchen and Kate's in the living room. Come on or they might think we're hiding from them.' She took his hand and they went to the living room.

'So it was you, Mr King. We thought it might have been my inspector. It's nice to see you. I'll leave you alone until my boss arrives,' said Kate.

He watched her leave and then asked Fiona, 'What's the inspector coming for? Has something happened?'

'Yes. We had a visit from a reporter on the *Gazette* earlier. I was praying that you wouldn't arrive while he was here.'

'What did he want?'

'He had heard about Reggie being killed and wanted to have an interview with his widow. How did he find out? I mean, who would have told him?'

'It must have been someone that was here on Saturday, I suppose. I was hoping the press wouldn't get on to it quite so soon. What did you tell the reporter?'

'I didn't see him. Kate and I stayed hidden while Mrs Romaine spoke to him at the door. She handled it very well. I was really proud of her.'

'So that's why the inspector's coming, is it?'

'Yes. Kate called him while Mrs Romaine was seeing if I was well enough to speak to him. He's coming back in the morning to get his story in before the national papers learn about it. My not being well and suggesting he came back tomorrow morning was Inspector Forward's instructions to us, via Kate. He should be here soon. Then we can relax. You will stay with me tonight, won't you?'

He smiled as he said, 'Razor, toothbrush, and toothpaste all present and correct, ma'am.' Then he whispered, 'But I forgot to bring my pyjamas. Should I go back and get them?'

A ring at the doorbell stopped her giving her reply. 'That will be the inspector. He knows you're here so you won't have to hide,' she said cheerfully.

Mrs Romaine showed the inspector to the living room, where Kate quickly joined them all.

'With your permission, your ladyship, I would like everyone to be seated so that we can all know what we're doing,' Bill said. He waited for them to sit before continuing. 'Now, this reporter calling has at least given you an advance warning of what to expect. The normal reaction of people being hounded by the press is to get away and hide from them. And that is perfectly natural. But in my experience, if you want to hide something the best place to leave it is on the table, which is the last place a burglar thinks of looking. And although you might wish to get away, m'lady, I would be happier if you stayed here. The last place a reporter would expect you to be. And if they are told that you've gone away they will believe it. Once the inquest and funeral are over, things will be easier for you.'

'Have you any idea how long that might be?' asked Edward.

'Not long, once our investigation is successfully completed. And I'm hopeful that will be reasonably soon, Mr King.'

'So you think you know who the killer is?' Fiona asked.

'We're gradually whittling them down, ma'am.' He turned to Mrs Romaine and took Farrow's photograph from his pocket. 'Was this the man that called to read the meter?'

Mrs Romaine looked carefully at the photograph and shook her head. 'I don't think so, Inspector. Even with a cap on I don't think this is the man.' She gave Bill the photograph back and said, 'I'm sorry. The man who came here was bigger and fatter in the face than this man.'

'Well, it was worth a try. Thank you, Mrs Romaine.' He then turned to Edward and asked, 'Do you intend staying here long, Mr King?'

Fiona was quick to reply. 'I have asked him to stay here again tonight, Inspector. I know it may appear very wrong to most people, but I need him with me. I was very nervous when that newspaper reporter came and although Mrs Romaine and Kate were here, I wanted Edward. I feel very safe when he's with me.' She took Edward's hand and held it as if proving her point.

'I can understand that,' said Bill. 'But the more often he's here, the more chance there is of somebody seeing him. And then the press could find out and make life very uncomfortable for both of you.'

'So what do you suggest we do?' asked Edward.

'As I see it you've got three choices. Either you only come after dark and leave at the crack of dawn, move in but stay out of sight, or keep away entirely,' said Bill.

Edward looked at Fiona with a smile. 'The first choice would fit perfectly with my new employment.'

'What new employment?' she asked.

'That was the news I wanted to tell you. Pinner and West are opening a new branch of their travel company in Fulham and have offered me the post of manager. It will mean just a short journey from here. And by the time the evenings start getting brighter all this business with the police will be over and you'll be able to decide where you want to live and do so in peace.'

Fiona was thrilled to hear the news of Edward's new job and had no intention of hiding the fact. Throwing her arms round his neck she said, 'Oh, Edward. You must be so pleased.'

'Yes, I am. And I'll be even more pleased if I don't choke to death before my first day,' he said, as he smiled and pulled himself free of her enthusiastic embrace.

'Congratulations, Mr King,' said Mrs Romaine.

'Yes, congratulations, sir,' said Bill Forward.

Kate echoed their good wishes and smiled.

'Thank you all. It will be nice to earn an honest living again,' said Edward. 'I'm lucky that an old colleague opened the door of opportunity for me. A man I used to work with recommended me.'

'Well, I'd better get back to my office before *I* have to look for a new job. Just remember to keep out of sight while you're here, Mr King. And you know what to do if the press bother you, m'lady. Remember you aren't feeling very well, so get tired and go for a lie down if the situation gets awkward. PC Weston will be around to give you any assistance you might need. Has anyone got any questions?'

'What do you want *me* to do if the press start calling here? Is there anything special I should say?' asked Mrs Romaine.

'Just try and protect her ladyship from anyone who is being too pushy or unpleasant.'

'Your reaction to Mr Korer was perfect today,' said Kate. 'I think he knew he'd met his match with you, Mrs Romaine.'

'Well, there you are. Good luck everyone. Hopefully we'll have our killer in custody soon.' Bill turned to Kate and said, 'You know how to reach me if there's a problem. I hope you will be able to return to your own place quite soon.'

'I don't mind staying here for a while longer, sir,' said Kate.

'Well, just remember. When anyone calls, keep your eyes and ears open.' He walked towards the door and said, 'We'll be off now. I wish you all a good evening.'

'I'll see you out, Inspector,' Mrs Romaine said and went out ahead of him.

Fiona looked at Kate and said, 'You'll have dinner with us again, won't you?'

'Are you sure I won't be in the way?'

'Of course you won't.'

'What *is* for dinner?' asked Edward.

'I don't know but Mrs Romaine will have something nice, I'm sure,' said Fiona. 'Would anyone like a drink?'

'I thought you would never ask,' Edward said with a grin.

When Bill got back to his office he was starting to feel tired and remembered Jane's warning about overdoing things.

'Anything happened while I've been gone?' he asked Marsh.

'The Kent boys have found Celia Benton and given us her phone number. She lives on her own in Maidstone. Do you want me to notify her of her cousin's death or will you do it?'

'You can give her a call now and see if she's prepared to arrange the funeral. Explain that she will require a certificate from the coroner's office before she can make arrangements and that she'll receive one in due course.'

Marsh dialled the number and waited, but there was no reply. 'She's not there. I'll try her again in the morning. How were things at Stafford House?'

'Her ladyship got nervous when the *Gazette* sent their man round to try for an interview. She only feels safe when Edward King is with her apparently. He's there now and staying the night again. I'm beginning to wonder if he's got other ideas now that the beautiful widow is getting to rely on him so much.'

'Ideas like getting his feet under the table, you mean?'

'Something like that, yes.'

'Well, it was you that told him it was all right to stay the night with her,' Marsh reminded him.

'I know. And then there's the housekeeper. I can't make up my mind about her. What I mean is, does she feel her nose is being pushed out of joint by Lady Fiona wanting King around so much? After all, Mrs Romaine practically ran the place with Sir Reginald being away all the time. Does she now sense Mr King's presence could be a threat to her position?'

'I hardly think he's going to take over running the place after only staying for one night.'

'It will soon be two nights, remember. Perhaps I'm getting too tired to think straight. Let's go home. We've done enough for one day. I'll see you in the morning. Good night, Marsh.'

'Good night, sir.'

Marsh watched him leave, realizing he was looking more tired than usual and hoped this case wasn't getting him down too much.

David Wilson had finished his early evening surgery and got home to find his wife sitting in the kitchen with a glass of white wine. She had not been feeling relaxed since her interview with Inspector Forward. When David appeared, she smiled and tried to look as though nothing was worrying her.

'Started without me, have you? I can't smell anything cooking. Have you gone on strike?' he joked.

Sara smiled. 'Yes, I'm on strike tonight, David. I thought we could go out and have a nice meal somewhere. I'm not in the mood for cooking.'

'Is something wrong? Are you feeling all right?' he asked.

'I'm fine. I just feel like a night out. Do you mind?'

'No. We'd better go somewhere that's in walking distance or I won't be able to have a drink.'

'I don't mind driving,' she said.

David pointed to her glass and said, 'Are you serious? We can walk to the French restaurant. Then I can have a drink here with you before we go. Will you book a table while I pour myself a drink?'

'OK. What time shall I book it for?'

David looked at his watch. 'About an hour if you want to eat early.'

Sara took the Yellow Pages from the shelf above the wall phone and started to turn the pages. David watched her and was puzzled.

'Why are you looking in the Yellow Pages? The number is in the local book.'

Sara realized she was looking in the wrong directory and gave a nervous laugh. 'Silly me. It must be the wine.'

'How many have you had?' he asked her. David opened the refrigerator door and took out an almost empty bottle of white wine as his wife became nervous. 'My God. This was a full bottle last night,' he said. 'Something's worrying you, Sara. What is it?'

'It's nothing, really,' she lied. 'I just fancied a glass of wine and must have had more than I thought. Sorry, David. I shall feel better when we've been out. Honestly.'

David still wasn't convinced but didn't pursue the subject. Instead he found the restaurant number and booked a table.

Bill Forward enjoyed being at home, having dinner with his wife. Jane had looked after him through all their married life together and understood his moods when he was worried about a case he was working on. He remembered Lady Fiona saying she felt safe when Edward King was with her. That's how he felt with Jane, safe and comfortable. He sat in his armchair after dinner and completely relaxed, putting the case at the back of his mind while he sat watching a comedy show on television. His eyes were beginning to close and he knew he would sleep better tonight and worry about the case when he felt fresh tomorrow.

CHAPTER SIXTEEN

M rs Romaine had arrived at Stafford House early, having slept in her own apartment again. She knew Edward King had left because she checked the cloakroom and saw that his overcoat had gone. Although she was pleased to see Fiona happy in his company, she did wonder if he was taking advantage of her. Fiona would become a wealthy woman after the death of her husband and Mrs Romaine worried that the money was Edward King's ulterior motive for befriending her ladyship. Mrs Romaine went to the kitchen and put the kettle on for Kate and Fiona's breakfasts. As she waited for the water to boil, she wondered how near the police really were to arresting the person they suspected of committing the murders of Philippa Pane and Sir Reginald. They seemed convinced that one of the guests on Saturday was responsible and she wondered who the prime suspect was. The fact that the inspector didn't appear to be worried about Edward King staying with Fiona overnight seemed to clear him of any suspicion. So who *did* they suspect? she wondered. And would Fiona move from the house and if so, would she still want a housekeeper? Her thoughts were interrupted by Fiona arriving and she was followed closely by Kate. Mrs Romaine made their tea and toast and took it to the breakfast room, where she left them to enjoy it.

'I didn't hear Edward this morning,' Kate said. 'So he must have left very early again.'

'I know. He was gone when I woke up. He's so quiet he'd make a good burglar,' laughed Fiona.

'He must be thrilled about his new job. I imagine he was a good manager where he was for these new people to grab him so quickly.'

'And to have a previous colleague recommend him shows he was popular with his staff. I'm so pleased for him,' said Fiona. 'He's a very nice, thoughtful man. Isn't it funny the way life takes you down an unexpected road? Here I am coming to rely on him and yet I've only really known him since Saturday. And I'm supposed to be in mourning for the man I married. A man I no longer have any feelings for. A man who turned out to be blatantly unfaithful to me, and who knows how many times he slept with other women.' She gradually became uncomfortable when she said, 'I suppose my sleeping with Edward makes me as unfaithful to Reggie as he was to me. But I was never ever unfaithful while he was alive. And that's the truth, Kate. You do believe me, don't you?'

'Yes, I do. But you mustn't feel too guilty. Your husband was obviously not a nice man, otherwise why would somebody want to kill him?' Kate realized she shouldn't have made that comment and quickly changed the subject. 'What was Edward like when you first knew him?'

Fiona said, 'Would you believe tall and skinny?'

'I can't imagine him being skinny. He certainly isn't now,' said Kate, smiling.'

'We were just teenagers then. Most boys seemed immature when they were teenagers.'

'They always had spotty faces as I remember,' laughed Kate.

'I don't remember whether he had a spotty face or not. But I do like the one he has now.' Fiona grinned.

'When does he start his new job?'

'He's going to collect the keys tomorrow to have a look round and get the feel of the place. He wants to see what office space there is, and work out where the desks will go, and all that sort of thing.'

Kate looked at her watch and said, 'You mustn't forget what Inspector Forward told you to do when the newspaper man gets here.'

'Oh Lord, I'd forgotten about him coming. I don't feel like talking to him. But if I don't, I suppose he'll make something up, just to sell the paper.'

'The inspector said you can always be too unwell to give him an interview. Anyway, he's not coming until eleven so you've got time to think about what you want to do,' said Kate. 'Mrs Romaine handled him well yesterday. I'm sure she can do the same today if you want her to.'

'Yes, she's very reliable. I shall really miss her if I have to move away.'

'I thought Edward didn't want to move away from this area because of his new job. I'm assuming you are including him when you talk about any plan to move away?'

Fiona was not immediate in her reply, which puzzled Kate for a moment.

'When I said I would miss Mrs Romaine if I moved away, I was referring to my intention of moving out of this house as soon as I can. I don't want to live here any longer than I have to, Kate. This house doesn't have particularly nice memories for me. I want to live somewhere nice where I can still see my friends. And yes, it would be nice to include Edward in any move I make. But I'm not stupid. I know that our relationship at the moment is mainly based on sex. I would like it to grow into something more stable and secure before I take a step that I might regret. So, at the moment, I shall leave things as they are and enjoy my life. Once the funeral is over I can make a decision on the future with a clearer mind.'

'Good thinking,' said Kate. 'And now what about enjoying another cup of tea before it gets cold?'

Ken and Angie Morris were finishing their breakfast when Angie brought up the subject of Saturday evening once more.

'I'm surprised the police haven't arrested anyone yet,' she said. 'I would have thought they'd have a good idea who killed Reggie by now. They know it wasn't us, or Paul and Sheila. Otherwise they'd have taken us in. Who do you think it was, Ken?' He was about to finish a mouthful of fried egg to answer, when Angie continued, 'I still think that man Philippa brought – what was his name?'

Ken swallowed quickly in order to get a word in. 'His name was King. Edward King. Now can I finish my breakfast in peace please? It's no wonder I get indigestion.'

'It's the way you only half chew everything that gives you the indigestion.'

'That's because I don't get a chance to chew properly with you constantly going on about something,' he said. 'Now what were you going to say about the man Philippa brought?'

'Well, I think he could be more sinister than he appears. He *was* an unexpected guest, remember. And now she's dead as well. And what do we know about him? I'll be surprised if he isn't involved somehow. Shelia thinks he's suspicious too.'

Ken laughed and said, 'You two would get any man hung if you didn't like him. Suppose the housekeeper did it instead of the butler? Then she could kill Fiona and run off with

Edward King and marry him because he's really her secret lover. That's after they'd got Fiona's money, of course. Have you thought of that possibility?'

'It's all right for you to laugh but I bet that Edward is in it up to his neck and just taking Fiona for her money. You only have to look in his eyes to see there's something shifty about him.'

'Perhaps he wants to kill me and run off with *you*. Had you thought of that?' Ken said with a serious expression. 'After all, you have got lovely legs and that might be what turns him on.'

'If you don't want to be serious I'll go and wash up.' She began to clear the table while Ken sat in another chair and picked up the paper. He hid behind it as she started speaking again. 'Most husbands don't like to see their wives ruining their hands with detergent and washing-up water. They buy them a dishwasher,' she said, intending it as a hint.

She was walking towards the kitchen carrying the dirty plates when Ken called after her. 'I bought you some rubber gloves. What more do you want?' he joked.

He was grinning as he hid behind the paper, expecting a rude retort from her, but there was no reply. Grateful for the silence, he relaxed and carried on reading. After a few moments, Angie came back looking thoughtful and sat down again.

'Ken, I've just remembered something that Sheila told me Philippa said to her.'

Putting his paper down he said, 'Oh, please, love, not Philippa again. The poor woman is dead, so give it a rest, eh?'

'She told Sheila that she believed Reggie's murderer was the last person anyone would suspect. And that Fiona was in for a nasty shock. Now what do you think she meant by that?'

Ken put his paper down and showed his frustration at

trying to read. 'She was a troublemaker who loved to draw attention to herself and if she was telling people what she told Sheila, I'm not surprised someone killed her. And now I'll go to my office, lock the door, and try to read my bloody paper in peace and without hearing any more about Philippa.' He got up and walked out of the room, leaving Angie wondering what she had done to annoy him.

Bill Forward arrived at his office feeling refreshed after a good night's sleep. He was going over the case in his mind as Marsh walked in.

'Good morning, Marsh. I trust you slept well.'

'Yes, thank you, sir.'

'Good. I want you to sit down and go over something with me.'

'What's that, sir?'

'We know that Tony Farrow intended to blackmail his father by fair means or foul and screw him for all he was worth.'

'According to Sara Wilson, yes,' Marsh agreed.

'Now according to the maitre d' at the White Hart in Dorking, Sir Reginald was having his way with a young blonde prostitute at night. Well, Mandy Lucas is a young blonde who was, and might still be, a prostitute. Now do you see the possible connection with Farrow?'

'You mean once he'd got evidence that his father was paying a prostitute at the hotel, he could blackmail him for a small fortune, will or no will.'

'Yes. Sir Reginald wouldn't have wanted his young wife or business associates to know what he was up to. He'd risk becoming a joke and he wouldn't have liked that,' said Bill.

'And Mandy would give Farrow any alibi he wants. But hang on a minute. We know he wasn't involved in Sir Reginald's murder because he was in Wales when that happened. In any case, why would he kill the goose that lays the golden egg? It doesn't make sense,' said Marsh.

'I know. And that was the one thing that worried me. You see, we've been assuming all along that Farrow was where he and Mandy told us he was. But how do we know he really was in Wales? This cousin of his might be a complete phoney and I don't want to fall for one of Farrow's con tricks and be made to look a fool. Get Farrow's photo down to the constabulary at Cardiff and ask them to check whether he was staying at the cousin's address. Always assuming there *is* a cousin and not someone who's in some sort of scam with Farrow. The local lads will be able to check that out. I still can't help feeling that we might be falling for exactly what Farrow wants us to. Anyway, once the Welsh lads have checked I shall know if he's involved and if he is then we can put pressure on him.'

'I'll get the photo off to Cardiff right away.'

'Good lad.'

Doctor David Wilson picked up his morning delivery of mail from the doormat.

'Is there anything for me?' Sara called from the landing.

David looked quickly through the envelopes. 'Just one. Looks like it was sent to the wrong address and has been re-addressed to here,' he said, studying the envelope. 'Do you want me to bring it up?'

'No, it's all right. I'm coming down.'

Sara came down wearing her dressing gown and took the letter from him. 'Good grief!' she said as she recognized the handwriting.

'What is it?'

She stood staring at the envelope in disbelief. 'It's from her.'

'Who?'

'Philippa Pane!'

David took the envelope back and looked at it again. 'Don't be silly. How can it be?'

'I tell you it is. I'd know her handwriting anywhere.'

'Well, don't just stand there, Sara. Open it and see what it says.'

Sara wished she hadn't told David who the letter was from and because she was frightened of its contents, pretended she was pulling his leg. She gave a laugh and said, 'I'm only joking, David. It's from the lady I went to see about making some new spare room curtains. You should have seen your face, though.'

'Well, it was a bloody shock. You gave me the heebie-jeebies. I'll be off now. I have a surgery to do. And next time you see your curtain lady, give her our correct address. Bye, love.'

She waved him goodbye and then opened the letter from Philippa. It was written and posted on the morning of the party at Fiona's. It said:

Dear Sara, I believe you visited a mutual male friend in Dorking and from what I gather you had a wonderful time with him. I'm assuming you would like to keep your physical activity with him strictly private and so I think we should meet and discuss it, don't you?
Yours, Philippa.

Sara went cold as she wondered what Philippa was intending to do when she wrote the letter. Was it blackmail she had in mind or something other than getting money? Sara couldn't think straight and decided to burn the letter and forget about it. After all, she reminded herself that Philippa was dead and couldn't do any harm now, whatever her intentions were. It was after the letter was put on the fire that Sara had another thought. Could it be possible that it was Philippa who killed Reggie? But then Sara knew she was being stupid. After all, it was surely the same person who killed Philippa that killed Reggie. Even so, she wished she could tell someone about the letter but she knew that was impossible. Otherwise everyone would know what only the police knew about her visits to the hotel at Dorking. That was something she would never want divulged.

CHAPTER SEVENTEEN

The morning post had arrived late and when Mrs Romaine picked it up she was intrigued to see one letter from the coroner's office. She took the letters to Fiona, who was talking to Kate in the breakfast room.

'Sorry to bother you, my lady. The post just arrived and I've noticed one is from the coroner's office. It might be important.'

Fiona took the letters and opened the official one first and read it aloud. 'It says an opening inquest is being held the day after tomorrow and I'm requested to attend.' She turned to Kate and asked, 'What is an opening inquest?'

'It's just to officially establish the identity of the deceased by his next of kin,' Kate told her. 'You only have to say that the person was your husband and give his name and date of birth. And that's usually all there is to it.'

'Is that all?' Fiona asked. 'It seems a waste of time.'

'Does nobody else have to be there?' asked Mrs Romaine. 'Only it was me that found Sir Reginald when I went to make the fire up.'

'The only other person would be the pathologist who's done the post mortem, and once the brief hearing is over, the coroner can give permission for the funeral to take place,' said Kate. 'It's usually very quick and straightforward.'

Mrs Romaine looked relieved at not having to attend the inquest and left the room.

'I shall be so glad to get the funeral over with. It's like having a cloud hanging over me at the moment,' Fiona said. She was about to say something else when the front doorbell rang and she listened to see who it was. She heard Mrs Romaine and Simon Korer's voice. 'Oh damn. It's that dreadful reporter. He's the last person I want to see. Never mind. I'll get rid of him as soon as I can,' Fiona whispered. She went into the hall and put a smile on her face.

'It's the gentleman from the *Gazette*, my lady,' said Mrs Romaine.

'Good morning, Mr Korer. Can you be as quick as possible as I have the doctor coming to see me soon,' Fiona lied. 'Come into the living room, won't you?'

Simon Korer followed her and said, 'Thank you, my lady-ship. I shall not take up much of your time.' He tried to sound as though he was used to speaking to titled people.

Fiona was about to close the living-room door when she signalled for Mrs Romaine to ring the doorbell in fifteen minutes' time. Her housekeeper gave an affirmative nod to show that she understood, and returned to the kitchen.

'Do sit down, Mr Korer,' said Fiona.

'Thank you, my ladyship.' He sat in an armchair and got his notebook ready. 'Have the police any idea who killed your husband? Or are they grasping at straws, would you say?'

'I'm not privy to their knowledge,' she replied. 'But I am sure they will soon apprehend the person that carried out such a terrible act.' She chose her words carefully so as not to give him a stupid reply that he could quote.

'Got someone in mind, have they?' he asked, with his pen ready to write her reply.

'I'm sure they have an idea. Our police are more efficient

than they are sometimes given credit for. Don't you think?' Fiona said.

'Oh yes, they aren't all thick, I give you that. So how was it done? Knife, gun, strangled, poison, what?'

'It was none of those, Mr Korer. We think he was hit with a weapon of some sort.'

'Think? You mean they're not sure! You must be joking.'

'I have just lost my husband, Mr Korer. And the last thing I want to do is joke, I assure you.'

'Oh, I wasn't suggesting otherwise, my ladyship.'

His obvious ignorance annoyed her and she felt the need to correct him. With a calm smile she said, 'The way to address me is "your ladyship". Not "*my* ladyship".'

He obviously knew he had been put in his place and looked slightly annoyed as he said, 'Yes, of course. So how was your husband killed?'

'As I just informed you, he was struck with something. And the blow killed him.'

'But do they know what he was hit with or is it still a mystery to the police?'

'I really don't think I can answer that. I reiterate, I am not privy to their knowledge. Why don't you ask them?'

'All they'll say is no comment. Getting information from the police is like squeezing blood from a brick.' He changed tack and asked, 'I believe you had a party going on Saturday night, so who was it that found your husband?'

'My housekeeper. She went to check the fire and discovered him in his study. The poor woman had a terrible shock, as you can imagine.'

'You didn't find him first then. It was the housekeeper.' He was writing as he went on, 'When did you know he was dead?'

'She called me immediately she found him. It was awful.'

'So your husband didn't join in the party then? He stayed

in his study. A bit unusual to be in the study when he's got guests, isn't it?'

He was starting to irritate her. 'My husband had some very important business papers to go through before joining us.'

'A little bird tells me that your husband was not the most popular man around. And that he was a lot older than you. Anyone can see why he was attracted to *you*, but what made you marry *him* if he was like they say? Was it the money?'

She snapped. 'I think I shall call a halt to this and see you out.' She went to the door and held it open for him to leave.

'I understand your husband was not liked much. Is that true?' he repeated as he got to his feet.

Ignoring him, Fiona went to the front door and opened it. Realizing he wasn't going to get any more from her, he reluctantly left the house. Mrs Romaine heard the door slam and came to see what had happened.

'I've just thrown that horrible man out. I couldn't take any more of his unpleasant questions. If any other members of the press come here, I'm not here. I've gone away,' Fiona told her.

'Yes, I understand.'

Kate came and gave an enquiring look. 'What happened?'

'Come into the living room and I'll tell you. Could we have some coffee, please, Mrs Romaine?'

'Of course.'

Fiona and Kate went into the living room while Mrs Romaine went to make the coffee for them. She was hoping Fiona hadn't given Mr Korer reason to print something scandalous that might affect *her* privacy as well.

Terry Kennedy called at the police station on the off chance that Inspector Forward might be there. Sergeant Cooper knew who Terry was and that the inspector would be pleased to see him. Knowing Bill was in, he escorted Terry straight up to the office, knocked and opened the door.

'Sorry to bother you, sir,' said Sergeant Cooper. 'You've got a visitor.' He smiled and showed Terry in, then left.

Bill and Marsh looked to the door and saw Terry enter with a big smile on his face.

'Hello, Mr Forward. Hello, Sergeant Marsh.'

Bill got up and greeted him. 'It's nice to see you, lad.'

Marsh gave a wave and said, 'Welcome back to the land of the living, Terry.'

'Sit down, lad,' said Bill, offering him a chair. 'They let you go this morning then?'

'Yes. They said I'd be fine as long as I take things easy for a while. But I wanted to see you and the bus doesn't take long from the hospital to here. I enjoyed the journey.'

'You mustn't overdo it on your first day out of hospital. But it's very nice to see you up and about again. You gave us a scare, you know. Does Father O'Connor know you're discharged?' Bill asked.

'Yes. I phoned him just before I left hospital. He was pleased I was coming out. He said he'd phone you but I asked him not to. I wanted to surprise you.'

'Well, you certainly did that, lad.'

'I know who it was that beat me up now. One of the boys from the club came to see me and said the one who did it was Jeff Donaldson.'

'You mean Mark Donaldson's boy?' asked Bill.

'Yes. Do you know him, Mr Forward?'

Bill looked at Marsh and said, 'Mark Donaldson was done for drugs last year. Dave Norris was the arresting officer. He came to see me the other morning but I was with Father O'Connor when he popped in, remember?'

'Oh, yes. The inspector you were at Hendon with,' Marsh said.

'That's him. He caught Donaldson when they raided his home and found fake passports and thousands of forged ten and twenty pound notes he was getting ready to circulate.' Bill turned back to Terry and said, 'So it was his boy Jeff that beat you up?'

'I said whoever did it was probably after money for drugs. Well, from what I gather, he's on crack,' Terry said.

'I can get someone from our drug department to check him out,' said Bill.

'Don't do that, Mr Forward. He'll put two and two together and might pay me another visit,' said Terry nervously.

Bill sighed. 'What a world we live in. Our decent young-sters who do everything to be law-abiding citizens are frightened to upset a minority who are on drugs and booze.' He gave Terry an understanding pat on the shoulder. 'Don't worry lad. I'll not get you into trouble with Donaldson. Now tell me what you're going to do. Take it easy for a while, I hope.'

'Yes, I will. But I had another reason to come and see you, Mr Forward.'

'What's that, lad?'

'We're having a raffle at the club and wondered if you'd like some tickets?' said Terry, producing a book of tickets.

'Well, now, that depends on two things, lad,' Bill said with a straight face.

'What's that?' asked Terry.

'The price of the tickets and the prize I might win.'

Terry realized Bill was teasing him and said with a smile, 'They're ten pence each, or fifty pence for a strip of six. And there are three prizes – a portable radio and disc player, three videos of your choice and a large box of chocolates. And

I think Father O'Connor is adding a mystery prize. We're calling it a mystery prize because he isn't sure whose arm he can twist to give us something.'

'Well, I think Sergeant Marsh would buy some tickets. He's very fond of chocolates, aren't you, Sergeant?'

'Yes. I could do with putting on some weight. I'll have five pounds' worth,' Marsh said as he took a note from his wallet.

Terry was surprised and looked delighted. 'That's very kind of you, Sergeant.'

'Well, my wife will want me to get some tickets for her, so I'd better have five pounds' worth for her, as well as five for me,' said Bill as he took a ten pound note from his wallet.

'Thanks, Mr Forward,' said Terry, grinning from ear to ear.

'What's the money in aid of?' asked Marsh.

'Father wants to get some things to make our club more up to date. And the builders yard are getting us paintbrushes and emulsion to clean the inside with. If it's nicer inside the boys will look after it more.'

'Well, you've got to hand it to Father O'Connor. He's kept you lads out of trouble and given you a purpose in life, rather than see you on drugs and getting into trouble all the time. He's a good man,' Bill said. Then he joked, 'I hope he isn't using money from the collection box to buy *his* raffle tickets.'

Terry laughed and put the raffle tickets in his pocket with the money.

'Mind you don't get mugged on the way back,' Marsh said.

Terry was about to leave when Bill asked him, 'How many more tickets have you got on you?'

'I've got another two books,' Terry answered.

'Well, leave one with me and I'll get the lads here to buy a few,' said Bill.

'Thanks a lot, Mr Forward.' He took a new book from his pocket and gave it to Bill. 'I hope they buy some from you.'

'Oh, they will.' He winked. 'Off you go and don't forget what they told you. Take it easy for a day or two. And give my regards to your aunt.'

As Terry left the office, Bill tossed the raffle book over to Marsh and said, 'Ask that nice PC to get me a coffee. And sell her some of these while you're smiling at her, eh? Otherwise I might have to put an adverse report on her application form for promotion, which I received this morning.' He waved a form in the air to prove he had it on his desk.

Marsh went to the hall and saw the girl he liked. After a brief word she confirmed that she had applied for promotion and Marsh returned to his desk.

'Your coffee will be on its way. And she'll get rid of some tickets for us.'

'Good girl. If you'd known young Terry's father you would be so grateful at the way the lad has turned out. A real villain his father was. I'm not particularly religious and I'm not Catholic, but I tell you this, Father O'Connor has done wonders with those lads at his club. He's been more like a father than their real ones, I can tell you,' Bill told him.

'Do you mind if I ask you a question, sir?'

'Go ahead.'

'Well, you mentioned an application for promotion just now. And I was wondering why you haven't been made up to chief inspector yourself.'

Bill gave a gentle laugh and said, 'I often get asked that. And the answer is very simple. I was offered promotion a while ago, but there was a problem. It would have meant my moving to another metropolitan area. You know the way you were moved to Chelsea. Well, when you're young it goes with the job. You move on, get a bigger pension and retire still reasonably young and get a job with a security firm or something similar. But when I was made up to inspector I applied to move from Hackney to Chelsea. Jane and I had friends from this area and we both liked Chelsea. My wish was granted and I came here. But if I'd gone for another pip on my shoulder I wouldn't have stayed here. I'd be moved on again, to God knows where. So Jane and I talked it over and because we weren't relying on my police pension to see us into our old age, I decided to stay put and see my time out here in Chelsea. Can you understand that?'

'Yes. I suppose once you're married you don't want to keep moving about. And that's a nice house you and your wife have. If I lived there I wouldn't want to move.'

'That's the way we feel, sunshine. There's no point trying to get more when you might end up with less. Happiness and peace of mind are more important when you get older.'

Marsh hesitated before saying, 'I've never mentioned it before, but when I first came here someone said you had a son in Australia. Is that true, sir? Only you've never mentioned him.'

Bill chuckled as he answered. 'I've never mentioned him because I don't have one. I know the story went round but that was because we looked after the boy of a friend of mine for a while. He and his wife went down with a virus and wanted the lad kept out of the way for a while in case he caught it. Jane and I had the boy with us for nearly a month and sometimes I would get him from school and bring him back here with me until it was time to take him home. When someone asked who he was I said it was my son, for a joke, that's all. Anyway, his parents had planned to emigrate to Australia and when they were fit and got things sorted out that's what they did. And that's how the rumour about my son got started.'

'So you didn't have any children of your own then?'

'No. Nature can be very unkind to some women and

prevent them from becoming mothers. But we don't really mind now. We've got each other and complete freedom.' He cleared his throat and said, 'And now I think we should do what we're being paid to do, don't you?'

'Yes, of course,' Marsh said, somewhat awkwardly.

'Right, first of all I'd like to know where my coffee has got to.'

Marsh got up and went to the door. 'I'll chase it up. She's probably selling those raffle tickets and it's delayed her.'

As Marsh left, Bill sat thinking about the boy and his parents in Australia, and decided to send an email to them.

By the time Marsh got back with the coffee, Bill had written the email and was ready to send it. Marsh put the cup on the desk and said, 'She said sorry it took so long. But she did manage to sell all but six strips of the raffle tickets. And you won't believe who she sold four strips to,' Marsh said with a grin. 'She only went to Superintendent Lamb's office.'

Bill was surprised and said, 'Well, if she got twenty quid from him, I shall personally recommend her for promotion.' He drank his coffee and smiled. 'Young Terry will be pleased at the speed we got his tickets shifted. Thanks for asking her to do that, Marsh. I appreciate it.'

'My pleasure, sir.'

'Let me send this email, then we must get back to business. It's a quick letter to my *son* and his parents in Australia. Just want to see how they all are.' He took an address from his notebook and sent the email. 'Well, that's that. Now, I wonder how long it will be before we hear from Cardiff?'

'Do you want me to chase them up?'

'Give them a bit longer. Tell me, if you had to pick one person as the number one suspect, who would it be?'

'At first I thought the doctor, because it seemed a bit too convenient him being there at the party. Then his wife admits she had sex with Sir Reginald and her story about the baby being adopted, it all began to look too contrived, I thought. But then there's Edward King. I can't make him out at all. Did that Philippa woman just happen to meet him or did he intend to meet her, so as to get into Stafford House and be with the girl he fancied as a teenager? Did Sir Reginald know who he was and confront him privately and end up dead himself? And what if her ladyship and King had arranged the whole thing in order to get her free? After all, they were alone downstairs before her husband was discovered dead. She could have arranged the cards to make King the detective and seem innocent of any involvement in her husband's death. Anyway, that's the way I see it at the moment,' said Marsh.

Bill had listened in disbelief. 'My question was, if you had to pick one person as number one suspect, who would it be? And you have just given me four! But you haven't even mentioned Tony Farrow. The man we think is the son of the victim and will possibly come into a lot of money.'

'Well, I'm still assuming he was in Wales when Sir Reginald was killed. But we'll have to wait for the Cardiff lads before we know for sure,' Marsh said.

Bill looked thoughtful and said, 'There are too many people in this mess. It won't be long before the *Gazette* print their story and then we'll really feel the pressure. I haven't heard from Kate Weston about any callers today, apart from the *Gazette*, that is. I'm surprised the party guests are keeping themselves away from Stafford House so much. I had expected them to be much more nosy as to what's going on, especially with Kate there. Patience is a virtue, they say. So we'll just have to be patient and see if it's true.'

Edward King's call to Stafford House was answered by Mrs Romaine, who put him straight through to Fiona.

'Hello, gorgeous.' He spoke in that warm voice she loved to hear.

'Hello. Do I know you?' she teased. 'Are you the burglar that crept out of my bedroom without waking me?'

'That's me,' he said. 'But I didn't take anything.'

'Nothing?' she asked provocatively.

'Only what I was given, willingly,' he whispered. 'How long have you been up?'

'Ages. I'm glad you called. Kate and I had breakfast and now I'm sitting here all alone and wondering what you're doing.'

'Apart from thinking of you, I was wondering if I should burgle you again tonight.'

'Oh, yes, please.'

He had a laugh in his voice as he said, 'You're incorrigible.'

'I know.'

'I'm getting the office keys a day earlier, so I shall go and have a good look round later.'

'Oh, that's good. Then you can tell me all about it tonight. Oh, and by the way.'

'Yes?'

'That man from the *Gazette* came. He's a completely nasty piece of work. I managed to be pleasant, I think. But then I had to cut the interview short. God only knows what lies he will write.'

'When does it come out?' he asked anxiously.

'Tomorrow morning or it might be tonight. I never read it so I'm not sure. I'll ask Mrs Romaine. She reads it I think.'

'Did he mention me?'

'No. Don't worry. If he had known you were staying overnight here he would have certainly asked about you. I think we've managed to keep you well hidden so far. Be careful when you come tonight, won't you?'

'Of course I will. I'd better go. See you tonight.'

Edward hung up, hoping Fiona was right about the reporter not knowing he was sleeping there. The last thing he wanted was for his plans to be ruined by a local rag.

The call from the Cardiff constabulary was put through to Marsh, who signalled Bill to pick up the extension.

'DS Marsh.'

'This is Sergeant Long, regarding your request for the check on Tony Farrow.'

'Yes?'

'Well, according to his cousin, Barry Evans, he was here on the date you gave us then left to do a tour of Wales. When we tried to get the number of the car he was supposed to have hired, Barry Evans couldn't give us any details. So we got in touch with all the local car hire places. We showed them Farrow's photograph but none of them had let out a car to a Tony Farrow, or Barry Evans. We went back to Barry Evans' place and got him to let us in. It's a small cottage with only one bedroom. So if Farrow stayed there he must have slept on the floor, the armchair, or shared a single bed with Evans. It's only a weekend place he lives in. I got the feeling he was lying about Farrow visiting him. We even went to the coach station but no one there recognized Farrow either.'

'Well, thanks for your help,' said Marsh. 'We really appreciate it.' He hung up and looked at Bill. 'So it looks as though Farrow has been giving us a cock and bull story all along.'

'Yes. And now we need to have a word with Mr Farrow. But before that, I want to see what Mandy Lucas has got to say. I have a feeling she'll respond to a bit of pressure,' said Bill. 'You've got her home number there. Give her mother a ring and see if she's there. And if she is, hang up and go and fetch her back here. I don't want her talking to Farrow before we get the truth from her.'

Marsh looked up the number and dialled. 'Hello. Can I speak to Mandy, please?'

'This is Mandy.' When the line went dead she thought it was a client and that the man would ring back.

Marsh put the receiver down and got up. 'She's there. I'll be as quick as I can.'

As soon as Marsh left, Bill went straight to Superintendent Lamb's office.

'Come in, Forward. What news?'

'I'm bringing Mandy Lucas in for questioning. I want her answers recorded so I'll take her to an interview room.'

'She might insist on a solicitor, so be prepared for that,' said Lamb. 'May I ask how she's involved in the Pace-Warren case?'

'We think she's on the game and was set up by Farrow to get into bed with Sir Reginald as a client at a Dorking hotel.'

'Who else knows about this?'

'The maitre d' at the hotel for one.'

'One's enough. It's all the press would need. Anyone else?'

'Ken Morris and Paul Robson, two of the guests at the party on Saturday night, knew Sir Reginald had a blonde with him in his room at Dorking. But they didn't know the girl in question. They got their information from the maitre d' so he's obviously been talking.'

'You must make it clear to her that she's not being arrested. Going to an interview room might suggest other-wise and we want her to talk, not get frightened and start asking for a solicitor. You see what I'm saying.'

'Point taken, sir. I'd better go. Marsh should have her here soon.'

'Good luck, Forward, and thanks for the up-date.'

Bill left the superintendent's office and walked briskly back to his own.

Marsh was on his way through the traffic with Mandy sitting nervously in the back of the car, wondering what was going on. Marsh explained why she was going to the police station. 'The inspector just wants a word with you. But he can't leave the station at the moment. Just relax and enjoy the ride. I'm a lot cheaper than a taxi,' he joked.

It was just half an hour to the station and Mandy was taken straight to the interview room and was starting to tremble as she sat at the long table and waited. Finally Bill Forward came.

'I've ordered some tea for you. It will be here in a minute. Now, Mandy, you were seen at a hotel in Dorking on more than one occasion with Sir Reginald Pace-Warren, and I would like to know what you were doing there and why you were with that particular gentleman. And I must warn you that I know you lied to me about Farrow being in Wales, so let's start telling the truth, shall we?'

Mandy was obviously thrown completely off guard and couldn't hide it. She tried to bluff her way out of trouble but was unconvincing. 'Well, no. I mean, I thought Tony *was* in Wales. Otherwise I would have said. And I only went to the hotel to get some money for my mum. I lost my job and we needed some money. She couldn't manage on a widow pension and my little bit of unemployment pay. But I didn't know who the man was, honest.'

'Are you saying that Farrow didn't tell you the name of the client he'd arranged for you?'

'Yes.'

'Yes he did or no he didn't?'

She became confused, 'Yes. I mean no, he didn't.'

'Mandy. I think he gave you the name of the man and made it clear that by your going to bed with him, Tony Farrow would be able to blackmail your client into paying a lot of money to have his sexual activity with you kept very quiet.'

'We never ask the names of our clients,' she insisted. 'It's not done in my line of work. You know that Inspector.'

'Not their full name, perhaps. But when you first meet they give you a name. "Call me so and so", they say, don't they?'

'Oh yeah. They like you to sound familiar with them. It turns them on if you tell them they're great lovers while you call out their names and fake an orgasm.'

'So what did this client ask you to call him?'

Again she was thrown off guard and said nervously, 'I can't remember.'

'Such a short time ago and yet you can't remember?' Bill said. 'Well, let me help you, Mandy. "Call me Reggie." Isn't that what he said?'

She felt she had been trapped and was relieved to see the door open and a cup of tea brought in. 'I could just do with some tea,' she sighed. 'Gets warm in here, doesn't it?'

Marsh took the cup of tea and passed it to her as Bill watched her gulp it down.

'I needed that, I did,' said Mandy, trying to look relaxed. She asked, 'What was that name you said?'

'Reggie.'

She pretended to think and said, 'It might have been. I can't be certain, Inspector. A lot of water's gone under the bridge since then.'

'Yes. And a lot of clients have got into your bed, no doubt. Now you listen to me, young lady. I don't ask you these questions just to pass the time. The man you were faking your orgasms with is dead.'

Mandy was genuinely shocked. 'Dead!'

'He was murdered. So this is a murder enquiry. Now I shall ask you again. Was Reggie the name of the man?'

She knew it was pointless to lie. 'Yes.'

'That's better. And did Farrow tell you that the man was a relative?'

'No, he didn't! If that bastard has got me in the shit I'll kill him. I give you my word, Inspector, on my mother's life I never knew anything other than what Tony told me. And I believed him, silly cow that I am. He said he'd got a man lined up that would make us a fortune and all I had to do was spend a night or two in a hotel with him. He said he would arrange everything and for a few hours' work my money troubles would be over. And that's the truth. I swear it.'

'What about the story that Farrow was in Wales?' asked Marsh. 'We know he didn't stay at the address that he said he'd telephoned you from. The Cardiff police checked it out. So who was the man we spoke to?'

'The man who said he was Farrow when I phoned Cardiff on the number you gave me,' Bill added.

'Tony said it was his cousin. And that it was just to get the police thinking he was in Wales while he was doing something up here. A sort of joke, he said.'

'And what was the something he was really doing while we thought he was in Wales?' asked Marsh.

'He never told me what. Just that it was a lucrative deal but I don't remember what he actually said. At the time I didn't think it was anything to be worried about because he thought it was amusing that you thought he was in Wales. And I just thought it was another one of his get-rich ideas. Tony was always having ideas that he said would make money.' She looked mortified. 'When I think of the way he's got me involved in this, the bastard.'

'Lying to the police is a serious offence, Mandy. Do you

swear that what you are now telling me is the truth?' asked Bill.

'Yes, Inspector. It is, honest. But I've no idea what Tony was up to when he was supposed to be in Wales. I really haven't.'

'Well, there's one thing that we know happened around that time,' said Marsh. 'A certain gentleman named Reggie was killed in cold blood.'

'Bloody hell, this is getting like a bad dream. You think Tony killed the old man? Is that what you're saying?' asked Mandy.

'It's a possibility, don't you think?' Bill asked.

'Tony can be a rotten sod sometimes, I know that, but not a murderer. I can't see him killing anyone. No, sorry, I just don't believe he would do that,' she insisted. 'Look, I've slept with him and I refuse to believe I've had sex with a bloody murderer. I know he can be a callous bugger but Tony would never kill someone. I know him better than you do, Inspector. Trust me. Tony's not that evil.'

'He's not the nicest of men either. He was setting you up to go back on the game. And just when I thought you'd given up that kind of life. I'm disappointed in you, Mandy. And what would your mother think if she knew what you and Farrow were up to? Be proud of you, would she?'

Mandy panicked. 'Don't tell her, please. Promise you won't tell her.'

'Wouldn't she know what you've been doing if Farrow had screwed Reggie for the money as he'd planned? Or would you have told her you'd managed to get a job as the chairman of BP for a six-figure salary?' He showed her he was getting impatient as he said, 'Now where's Farrow?'

Mandy was getting uncomfortable. 'I don't know where he is right now. And I've no idea when I'll see him. Look, I've done nothing, so can I go home now?'

'If Farrow gets in touch with you, don't tell him about this chat we've had. Do you understand?'

'I won't say nothing. Honest I won't.'

'If he does call, find out where he is and let me know. If you don't you'll make me a very angry man and I shall have to tell your mother what you've been up to. Understand?'

'I'll do as you want, Inspector. I don't want to be mixed up in a murder. Can I go home now, please?' she nervously asked.

'For now you can. But I'll have you arrested and back in here faster than you can blink an eye if I find out you've lied to me.' He gave Marsh a nod and said, 'Get her out of here and take her home.' After Marsh had taken Mandy out of the room, Bill went to his office, wondering whether to send out an APB to have Farrow picked up. But he felt things were at last going his way and didn't want to make any mistakes.

When Marsh returned, he found Dave Norris from the drug squad in the office. The two men were laughing as Marsh walked in.

'Look who's dropped by,' said Bill

'Hello, Marsh,' said Dave. 'I hear you just took a young lady home. My governor doesn't give me those sort of perks, you lucky devil.'

Marsh smiled and said, 'And did he tell you she was on the game and that he knew her before I did?'

'I was trying to keep that a secret, Marsh. Now the whole station will know. And my affair with Mandy will come to a sad end,' Bill said. Then he asked, 'How was she on the way back?'

'Very quiet. I'm convinced you got her thinking seriously about her relationship with Farrow. With a bit of luck she *will* give us a bell if he gets in touch.'

Bill explained the case briefly to Dave Norris.

'He sound a nasty bit of work, this Farrow,' said Dave.

'Yes, he is. He's certainly messing up Mandy's life for her.' Bill took the opportunity of having Dave there and asked, 'Dave, can you do me a favour?'

'If I can.'

'A young friend of mine was beaten up by a boy on drugs. You remember Mark Donaldson?' said Bill.

'I should do. It was me that got him put inside.'

'Well, it's his boy Jeff that beat the lad up. He's on drugs, we understand, so he might be worth a visit.'

'I can certainly do that,' Dave said.

'Don't mention you got the tip from me. Young Donaldson will put two and two together and might go for revenge on my lad. I don't want him getting beaten up again.'

'Don't worry,' said Dave. 'I'll make it clear to him that we're following up a call we had from a lady who believes he's dealing drugs. Leave that to me, Bill. You never know, we might find out who his supplier is. They're the bastards *I* want put away.'

'Thanks, Dave. And good luck.'

'I'd better go. We're hitting a cabin cruiser when it comes in from Holland and I want to be there when it ties up. We've got a Dutch undercover man travelling with the craft's wealthy owner and his crew.' Dave looked at his watch. 'They should be coming in with over a ton of coke and heroin, so it will be nice to catch them as they start to unload. There's always someone who thinks they'll get away with it.' He shook hands with Bill and said, 'It's great to see you both. We'll go for a drink when I've sewn this case up.'

'Good luck with it, sir,' said Marsh to Dave.

'Thanks. And good luck with your Farrow enquiry. See you soon.'

Bill walked to the door with him and gave a good luck pat on his back. Marsh watched them, and thought it was nice that the two men had remained good friends over the years.

Kate Weston was in her bedroom with the door closed when she rang Inspector Forward.

'PC Weston here, sir.'

'Yes, Constable?'

'I thought you should know that Edward King has phoned to say he'll be back here tonight.'

'Getting to be quite a habit then?'

'Yes, and about the opening inquest in the morning, sir.'

'What about it?

'Do you want me to go with Lady Fiona, and if so, should I be in uniform?'

'I want somebody to be with her. I can't chance her going there alone.'

'The housekeeper said she would go with her if we wanted her to. On the other hand, Edward King might offer.'

'No. I definitely don't want King going. Have you got your other clothes with you?'

'No, sir. It was such a rush. And you wanted me to be seen in uniform by any callers. But it won't take me long to go home and change.'

Bill thought for a moment. 'You stay at the house. I'll come and take her there myself. I want to come back to the house anyway. There's something there that isn't quite right and I need to tie up some loose ends. Tell her ladyship I'll be over to collect her in the morning.'

'Right.'

As Bill hung up, Marsh looked over to him. 'Are these loose ends anything I should know about?'

'I'll have Lady Fiona to myself for a while when we go to

the inquest. It will give me a chance to talk to her without Edward King, Mrs Romaine and Kate being there. I'm hoping to find out if her ladyship knows more than she's told us about the death of her husband.'

'Do you think she's lied to us?'

'Not intentionally, perhaps. But I have a feeling she may have misunderstood what actually took place during her murder game. Something that actually happened, but she was too involved with her game to *realize* what had happened. And if I'm right, tomorrow could be our lucky day, sunshine.'

'Are you going to give me a clue, or do I have to wait till I read about it in the papers?' asked Marsh impatiently.

Bill wagged a finger and said, 'If I'm wrong you'll never let me live it down. And I won't be sure my hunch is right until I've spoken to Lady Fiona. Trust me a bit longer. If I'm right, you'll be the first to know.' He got up from his desk and went to the door. 'This calls for a coffee. Care to join me?'

Marsh smiled to himself, knowing his inspector was getting pleasure from teasing him. But he was curious to know what was going through Bill Forward's mind as the two men went to the canteen together.

Edward King was relieved that there was no *Gazette* on any of the news-stands. He was pleased the conversation at Stafford House wouldn't be all about any article in that paper. By the time it came out in the morning, he knew he would be away before anyone in the house had seen it. He was looking forward to being alone in the bedroom with Fiona again and wanted that more than anything. It was almost 5.30 in the afternoon and getting dark when he arrived at the house. Mrs Romaine opened the door and showed him into the television lounge, where Kate and Fiona were watching the local news. As he entered the room, Kate gave him a wave of acknowledegment as Fiona extended her hand and pulled him down to sit next to her on the settee.

'We won't be a minute, Edward. We're just watching to see if they say anything about our Saturday drama,' she whispered.

Edward nodded and sat holding her hand, watching the news with them until it finished. 'Thank goodness there was nothing on there about us,' Fiona said with relief as she got up and turned the television off.

'Did you really expect there to be?' asked Edward.

'We wondered if that *Gazette* reporter might have been talking,' said Kate.

'I doubt it. He wanted his story to be an exclusive,' Edward reminded them.

'We thought we would check the news anyway, just in case,' Fiona said. 'There'll be some tea coming in a minute. Shall we stay here and have it?'

'Yes, this is a comfortable room,' Edward said as he looked around. 'Do you often use it?'

'I used to when Reggie was away. The television was the only company I had sometimes, unless my friends came round, or I went out to see them.'

Mrs Romaine came in with a tray of tea and a homemade cake. 'This is a fruit cake I made this afternoon. I hope no one is allergic to nuts, only there are some chopped almonds in it.'

'I'm not,' said Edward, his mouth watering.

'Me neither,' said Kate.

Mrs Romaine smiled at Fiona, 'I know you aren't, my lady. You've had it many times before.'

'I'm never allergic to anything *you* cook, Mrs Romaine,' said Fiona.

Mrs Romaine left the room feeling pleased with herself.

'I'll have my tea then be out of your way,' said Kate.

'Don't be silly. You aren't in our way. Sit and relax,' Edward told her. 'In any case, I want to tell you about my new offices. One day, Kate, you might even want to book a holiday with me. I'll give you a discount if you bring your boyfriend with you. Or even a girlfriend or member of your family. The company allow me to give discounts at my discretion, so remember that.'

'I certainly will.'

Edward went on enthusing about his new position while Kate and Fiona sat listening to him. Fiona wondered what it would be like if she was with Edward on a regular basis. She liked him a lot and loved being in bed with him. But she tried to imagine them as a couple after the sexual desire had lost its novelty and become less frequent. Would she still feel safe and comfortable with him or would she regret allowing him into her life? Looking at him and listening to him talking about the new job, she was aware of her feelings for him and knew it would be hard to be without him, especially right now.

Inspector Forward was attempting to draw a plan on a piece of paper when he looked thoughtful and said to Marsh, 'Can you describe the ground floor of Stafford House from memory?'

'I think so. Why?'

'Tell me the layout, starting from as you come into the front door.'

Marsh thought for a moment and said, 'Turning left you've got the cloakroom. Then the television lounge. That's almost next to the kitchen. Oh, then that small breakfast room with a door leading to the dining room. Am I right so far?'

Bill looked at his plan and said, 'I'd forgotten the door from the breakfast room to the dining room.' He marked it down and said, 'Carry on.'

Marsh continued. 'Next to the dining room you've got the living room. Then the staircase, at the bottom of which, on the right, is the study. Then you're back to the front door again. Oh, there's the back door from the drive to the kitchen and the garage. I think that's about it.'

'Thank you, Marsh. That's exactly what I've got down, and in the morning we shall see if either of us missed anything. I'm looking forward to seeing Lady Fiona. Then you and I can carry out an experiment. You can get off home when you're ready.'

After Marsh had left, Bill sat for a moment, going over details of the case. Before he left the office, he decided to make a call to David Wilson. It was Sara who answered.

'Inspector Forward here, Mrs Wilson. Is the doctor there?'

'His surgery doesn't finish until five thirty, Inspector. He gets home after six usually.'

'I shall be gone by then. Tell him I shall be at Stafford House after I bring Lady Fiona back from the opening inquest in the morning. I'll be there for a while from around eleven thirty, so if he could call in and see me I would be grateful.'

Sara became curious and said, 'Can I ask what you want to see him about? It isn't anything to do with my going to the Social Services, is it?' she asked, rather nervously.

'No, no. It's purely a medical question, Mrs Wilson. But you can come with him in the morning if you want to. Then you will know I won't be discussing your Social Services visit.'

Sounding relieved she said, 'Thank you. I shall pass your message on to David when he gets home.'

'I would appreciate it. Good day to you, Mrs Wilson.'

Bill hung up and wondered what Fiona would do if she knew that Sara had helped Reggie conceal the fact that he had a son who had encouraged a young girl to have sex with his father in order to blackmail him for money.

It was almost 7 p.m. when David Wilson returned home. He took his coat off and went to the living room and sat in his armchair. He was looking tired and Sara poured him a glass of whisky and took it to him.

'Thanks, love. I need that,' he said as he took the glass from her. 'It's been a lousy day.'

Sara poured herself a gin and tonic and sat with him. 'You relax and enjoy your drink.'

David sipped the whisky and sighed, 'I had that dreadful Mrs Chapman in today. She wanted to know if I could help her lose some weight. Stop eating so much, I told her. Cut out potatoes with meat and don't keep eating all those chocolates.'

'What did she say?'

'She gave the same excuse that all overweight people give. "It's the only pleasure I get nowadays." Well, she'll keep getting bigger till her heart packs up. And then Mrs Andrews asked if I could look at her daughter in the morning because she keeps losing her balance. She's a hypochondriac who is convinced she has an incurable disease. So tomorrow morning is going to test my professional expertise.'

'Oh, that reminds me. Inspector Forward would like to see you at Stafford House when you finish the morning surgery. He'll be there from eleven thirty, after he brings Fiona back from the opening inquest.'

David raised an eyebrow and asked, 'Why does he want to see me at the house? Did he say?'

'Something medical was all he told me,' she said.

'I wonder why he doesn't come to see me here or at the surgery?' David was puzzled as to why the inspector wanted him to go to Stafford House and wondered what his reason could be.

CHAPTER EIGHTEEN

Kate had gone to her bedroom to have a wash and tidy herself up before dinner, leaving Edward and Fiona sitting alone with a drink in the living room. Fiona put down her drink and told Edward about the inspector taking her to the opening inquest in the morning.

'I wonder why he wants to take you? Does he think you will get lost, or is he just a randy policeman that fancies you?'

'Don't be silly. He's worried about my going out alone until they catch the killer.'

Edward became serious and said, 'He's quite right, of course. You mustn't be left on your own until this murderer has been caught.'

Fiona pulled him closer. 'Isn't that why you are here, Mr King, to protect me?'

Taking her in his arms, they became locked in a passionate kiss. After a while their lips parted and Fiona said, 'God, I fancy you so much. I wish we were in bed right now.'

'Be patient,' he whispered. 'It isn't good to make love on an empty stomach.'

Her voice was soft and seductive. 'I wish that's where you were right now. My stomach and I would like that.'

'Not if Mrs Romaine walked in you wouldn't.' He smiled.

'She would probably be jealous. She might secretly fancy you herself,' Fiona whispered.

Edward laughed and said, 'Don't get me excited. I might run away with her.'

Fiona quickly put a finger to her lips. 'Keep your voice down. She might hear you.'

'Sorry. But seriously, what was her husband like?'

'I have no idea, I never met him. He had died by the time she came to work here. I really don't know anything about him as she never mentions him. And I get the feeling she doesn't want to. So I never bring up the subject.'

'He's a bit of a mystery then.'

'Yes. In a way, I suppose he is.'

'When she calls us for dinner I could ask her about him if you like,' said Edward. 'We might be surprised.'

Fiona shook her head. 'Not now. Once the funeral is over and we know what we're doing perhaps, but not now, Edward.'

'OK.' He shrugged. 'Whatever you want.'

Kate gave a gentle knock and looked in. 'Mrs Romaine asked me to tell you that she's about to dish up some food and is going to put it in the dining room.'

'Thank you, Kate. We'll finish our drinks and be right in,' said Fiona.

As Kate went, Edward whispered, 'I wonder what she wears in bed?'

Fiona gave him a playful slap. 'You're not supposed to wonder what other women wear in bed when you're with me.'

'Sorry, darling. It's just that every time I see her she's in her uniform. And I bet she looks nice in a dress.'

'You just called me darling!'

He looked at her and said, 'I believe that is the right way

to address the beautiful lady I go to bed with. The girl I think about all the time I'm not with her.'

She gave a loving look and said, 'It's the first time you have ever called me that, and I like it.' Her breathing became rapid. 'When we have had our food, you can take me upstairs and call me that as much as you like.' She kissed his cheek. 'Come on, before they send out a search party for us.' She took his hand as they walked to the dining room.

Mrs Romaine waited for them to sit down then served them neck of lamb and vegetables. 'In case you want some more, I shall leave the rest to keep warm in the oven.'

'Thank you. It looks lovely,' Fiona said.

'I'll be on my way now. See you in the morning,' said Mrs Romaine.

They said good night to her and started eating. But none of them knew that by this time tomorrow Kate Weston would not be with them.

Bill Forward got to his office early, having made a mental note of things he wanted to do this morning before taking Fiona to the opening inquest. He took Tony Farrow's photo from his drawer and put it in his pocket, along with the plan of the ground floor at Stafford House that he had drawn. It was just before nine o'clock when his phone rang. It was Fiona and she sounded anxious.

'I'm afraid Kate is unwell and wants you to know that she's going into hospital, Inspector.'

Bill was concerned and asked, 'What happened? What's the matter with her?'

'She woke up in terrible pain and I called Doctor Wilson. He came straight over and said it's her appendix. He called for an ambulance so it should be here any minute. I think someone should be with her.'

'I'll come right over and arrange a replacement for her. I don't want you even thinking of going with her if that's what you had in mind. Stay there, ma'am, and make sure you know which hospital they take her to. I'll see you in a few minutes.'

Bill was on his way out when he met Marsh coming in. 'Get someone over to replace Kate Weston. She's been taken ill and is on her way to hospital. I'll wait at the house until someone arrives and explain the situation to them. Just make sure she brings her uniform and overnight things with her.'

'Will you be back here before you go to the inquest?'

'I don't know. If I'm not, I'll see you at the house. Otherwise I shall ring you. I must dash.'

Bill hurried from the office, leaving Marsh wondering which of the policewomen he could send. He knew it had to be one like Kate, a woman with no ties at home. Sally Hamilton came to mind. Marsh was keen on her and he knew Bill was impressed at the way she sold the raffle tickets for him. And as she was applying for promotion, Marsh thought choosing her might give her that extra recommendation, and at the same time help him to have a closer relationship with her. He went to see if she was on duty, keeping his fingers crossed that she was.

By the time Bill Forward arrived at Stafford House, Kate had been taken to the Chelsea and Westminster hospital. Fiona was giving him details of Doctor Wilson's visit while he drank a fresh cup of coffee that Mrs Romaine had made for him.

'David said that it was her appendix and thought it would have to come out. The poor girl was in agony when he put pressure on that area.'

'I remember my wife was in agony before she had hers out. I shall go and see Kate as soon as we've been to the inquest.' Bill told Fiona.

'Someone should notify her parents but I don't know where they live,' she said.

'Don't worry. Our people have all the phone numbers and addresses for the next of kin of all the police officers, so they'll do that. Her replacement should be along fairly soon, then I'll put her in the picture.'

'I shall miss Kate.'

'No doubt you will. But I'm sure you'll like her replacement. I left it for Sergeant Marsh to arrange and if it's the girl that I think it will be, she's a very nice lady,' he said with a smile. 'By the way, have you packed Kate's things?'

'I'll go and do that right away, if you will excuse me.' She got to her feet and hurried upstairs.

Bill sat finishing his coffee as he watched her leave the room.

After a few moments, Mrs Romaine came and asked, 'Can I get you some more coffee, Inspector?'

'Thank you. That's lovely coffee.'

'It's freshly ground,' she proudly informed him. 'Oh and by the way, Inspector. I picked up the *Gazette* this morning and read the article by that Simon Korer.'

'And what did he say?'

'He spelt my name incorrectly, and refers to Doctor Wilson as Doctor Williams. The whole article is a load of rubbish. I have not shown it to her ladyship yet. But I don't think she will be too upset by it. I shall go and get you that coffee.'

'Thank you. But before you get the coffee, I wonder if you would do something for me.'

'Yes, if I can.'

'I will go into the cloakroom, and while I'm in there I'd like you to walk to the kitchen, wait a moment then walk to the study door. I want to try something and would appreciate your help, Mrs Romaine,' he said with a friendly smile. 'If you don't mind, that is?'

She was not sure what he was up to but agreed to do as he requested. 'No, of course I don't mind.'

'Thank you. I'll go to the cloakroom and when I close the door I'd like you to start,' Bill said.

He went into the cloakroom and closed the door firmly shut behind him. He listened for her movements but could only hear a faint suggestion of footsteps. He waited, and after what he considered to be enough time for her to walk back to the study, he opened the cloakroom door and saw her standing by the study door.

'Thank you, Mrs Romaine. I wasn't sure whether you had got back there or not. That cloakroom door is very thick, so it's not easy to hear through it.'

'Would you like me to do it again, sir?'

'No, thank you. But I would like that cup of coffee now.'

'I'll bring it to the living room for you,' she said.

Bill noticed her shoes as she left. They were ordinary flat heels with soft upper soles as he expected. He decided to try his experiment again later, but this time to see if he could hear Mrs Romaine scream, as she did when she found Sir Reginald's body on the night of the party.

Constable Sally Hamilton parked her car behind Kate Weston's in the driveway, wondering if it was the right place to put it. She took her suitcase from the boot and rang the front doorbell. Bill heard the bell and watched Mrs Romaine open the door. He was pleased to see the policewoman had arrived and went to meet her. Sally was twenty-three with a nice personality and Bill could see why his sergeant was so keen on the girl.

'Come in,' said Bill. 'This lady is Mrs Romaine. She is the

housekeeper and makes a delightful cup of coffee. So be nice to her.'

Sally smiled at Mrs Romaine and said, 'The inspector does like his coffee. But I've never heard him call one delightful before, so yours must be very special.' Then turning to Bill she said, 'I've parked behind Kate's car. Is that all right, sir?'

'It's fine. Put your case down and come into the living room. Then I can explain what I want you to do before I go back to the office. Lady Pace-Warren will be down in a minute. She's packing up Kate's things at the moment,' Bill said.

'Can I get you a coffee?' Mrs Romaine asked Sally.

'Thank you,' said Sally.

Mrs Romaine looked at Bill and said, 'I don't suppose I could interest you in another cup Inspector?'

'If it's half as nice as the last one, I would love one. Thank you.' He smiled.

As she went to the kitchen he showed Sally to the living room and they sat down.

'I was sorry to hear about Kate Weston, sir,' Sally said. 'She must have been happy here – it looks such a nice house. What's Lady Pace-Warren like?'

'She's very beautiful and Constable Weston got on well with her, as I'm sure you will. Now, your duty is to note who comes, even a casual caller. And let them see your uniform. We let it be known that there's a police officer here. It's important to keep her ladyship safe until the person that killed her husband is in custody. The same person appears to have killed another of the guests that were here on Saturday evening. So be careful.'

'I will, sir.'

Before Sally could ask anything else, Fiona arrived.

'I'm sorry I was upstairs when you arrived,' she said with a welcoming smile. 'I'm Fiona Pace-Warren.'

Sally stood up and introduced herself. 'Police Constable Hamilton, ma'am.'

'I called PC Weston Kate. What do I call you?'

'My name is Sally.'

'Then Sally it is. When you finish with Inspector Forward, I will show you to your room and you can get settled.'

'Thank you, ma'am,' said Sally.

'I shall be going soon, my lady. Then I'll be back to take you to the inquest,' Bill said.

'I'm grateful to you Inspector. I shall be glad when the funeral arrangements are over with. I will see you when you're ready, Sally,' Fiona said, and then left.

'I was right to call her ma'am, wasn't I, sir?' asked Sally.

'Yes, you were. Ma'am or my lady is correct.'

'I see what you meant about her being beautiful. She has a lovely face, and looks a lot younger than I had imagined.'

'Yes. But her husband was no oil painting. A strange man apparently, and according to her friends he was too busy making money and chasing other women to fully appreciate his wife,' said Bill.

Sally shook her head in disbelief. 'If I looked like her and my husband went after other women, I think I'd kill him,' said Sally.

Bill gave a smile and said, 'Somebody *did*. Let's go over what I want you to do and then I'll be off.' He looked at his watch as he added, 'I'll put Kate's suitcase in my car and take it to her on the way back from the inquest. It will give me a chance to see how she is.'

Bill gave Sally his instructions and left, taking Kate's case with him.

CHAPTER NINETEEN

When he got back to the office, Marsh was waiting to hear how he had got on with the replacement, Sally Hamilton.

'She's a bright girl without any ties so you made a good choice, Marsh.'

'Thank you, sir,' Marsh said, enjoying the compliment.

'But I wouldn't want to be married to her,' said Bill.

Marsh was surprised. 'Why?'

'She said if any husband of hers played around with other women she'd kill him. Oh, a dangerous woman is our Sally.'

Marsh realized he was being teased but decided to say nothing more about Sally Hamilton at the moment. Instead, he gave Bill news of Kate Weston.

'I had a call from Constable Markham at the hospital a few minutes ago. Kate had her operation soon after she arrived, so she should be out of the theatre any time. He's going to let us know how she is. Her family have been informed.'

'Good. I shall look in on her after I've been to the inquest.'

'What was the experiment you wanted me to do with you at the house?'

'I did it with Mrs Romaine's help. I may want to try it again when you're there. Then I shall be able to satisfy my curiosity about the footsteps in the hall.'

'I wish I knew what you were talking about.'

'It's a hunch really. Were the footsteps that Edward King and Lady Fiona heard when they were in the cloakroom those of Mrs Romaine, or somebody else's? Now if they were somebody else's, I want to know who that somebody was, because that person was more than likely the killer.'

'How are you going to find out? Get everyone to wear the shoes they wore on Saturday evening and ask them to walk across the hall?' Marsh said with a hint of sarcasm.

'Nothing so complicated, Marsh.'

'What then?'

'I'll let you know when I've worked that out.' Bill smiled. 'Has anything else happened that I should know about?'

'Yes. Mandy Lucas called to say that she thinks Farrow tried to telephone her then changed his mind. But she can't be sure it was him. Just a feeling she had that he heard her answer and decided not to say anything. If it was Farrow, he might have thought we've bugged her phone in order to track him down.'

'It could be.' Bill became thoughtful and said, 'I did wonder about having a bug put on the phones at Stafford House. But if Lady Fiona had found out we'd done so without her permission we could have been accused of invasion of privacy. It's a dodgy one, that is.'

'But surely she would have given permission?'

'Yes, possibly. But she might also have warned Edward King to be careful what he said to her over the phone, not wanting us to hear their private conversation. And that's two people too many when you're trying to catch a killer. In any case I don't think our people would have given us the go ahead unless we had a damned good reason to do so. There are too many possible suspects in this case. And there might even be a surprise one who is keeping their head down at the moment. And as long as they feel safe there's a good chance they'll slip up sooner or later and give themselves away.'

Marsh had a feeling there was someone special that Bill had in mind when he asked, 'Who's the surprise suspect? Doctor Wilson?'

Bill raised an eyebrow as he asked, 'Now what made you come up with him?'

'Well, being a doctor he's above suspicion, isn't he? We know his wife was having sex with Sir Reginald and that would give him the motive. Then there's the one person everyone feels sorry for and is probably the very last person anyone would suspect.'

'And who's that, Marsh?'

'Lady Fiona.'

Bill nodded in agreement. 'Yes, that's true. Is there anyone else you can think of?'

'There's our friend Tony Farrow, of course. We know he couldn't have grabbed Sir Reginald from the study window, but with his SAS training he might have got into the room and been waiting for his victim.'

'Ah yes, the mysterious Mr Farrow,' said Bill. 'But if he had got into the study and waited for Sir Reginald, surely Mrs Romaine would have seen him when she went in to make the fire? We know the room is small and saw for ourselves there was not really a place where he could hide.'

'But how do we know he didn't manage to get into the house unobserved and go to the study while everyone else was having their food in the dining room? He could have killed Sir Reginald in seconds and been gone before anyone knew.'

'That's a good point, Marsh. And if he came through that back door to the kitchen, Mrs Romaine could have been in the dining room, making sure everyone had enough food, so she wouldn't have seen him. Neither would anyone else.'

'It makes sense, doesn't it?' asked Marsh.

Bill checked his watch. 'I'd better be off to the inquest. And while I'm gone, apart from Farrow being the killer, see if you can think of somebody else that could have got into the study without being noticed.' He gave Marsh a wave and left.

Marsh watched him go and wished Bill had confided in him as to who he suspected. But he had learned that DI Forward liked to do things his way. And whoever the suspect was, he would only reveal their name when he was ready to do so, and positive he was right. Because if there was one thing Bill Forward hated it was being wrong.

CHAPTER TWENTY

Janet Davis had just got back from the supermarket and after putting her things away she went to see Andrew in his office.

'I've just met Angie Morris in the supermarket and she was saying how funny it is that we haven't been interviewed again.'

Andrew looked up from his desk and asked, 'Why should we be? We've told the police all we know.'

'Yes, but it is strange, isn't it?'

'What is?'

'Well, that policewoman is still with Fiona it seems. And that's a bit strange. I mean, the police must have an idea who killed Reggie but, as Angie said, they usually interview everyone again so as to check our stories. But they haven't done that and I agree with Angie, it's strange.'

Andrew laughed and said, 'How many murders has Angie been interviewed about? Or you, come to that? Have you been keeping your dark past from me all these years?'

'You can make fun of me if you want to, but Angie's got a good point. She thinks she knows who it is the police suspect, and you'll never believe who it is.'

'All right, surprise me. Who is it?'

'The lovely, gorgeous Fiona, that's who, and before you burst out laughing again, she could be right. Who else had a motive as obvious as Fiona? Reggie was at it with God knows how many women and what better reason could she have than that? She might have had enough and decided to put a stop to his philandering.'

Andrew gave her a look of despair. 'You and your women friends are the most dangerous people I know. One of these days you're going to get yourselves into a lot of trouble with your scandal-mongering. Why don't you leave it to the professionals to sort out who the murderer is and stick to what you know, rather than make up a lot of stories about our friends?'

'All right, but think about it, Andrew. Angie might be right and Sheila agrees. And now I shall go to the kitchen and make some cakes, like a dutiful housewife.'

She walked out, unable to hide her annoyance at Andrew's reference to her and her friends being scandal-mongers.

Sheila Robson was sitting in the kitchen with a cup of coffee and giving serious thought to Angie Morris's idea that Fiona probably killed Reggie as revenge for his womanizing. She wondered how she would react if Paul were to have an affair. Although he had the opportunity to do so when he went away to meet clients, she couldn't imagine him being unfaithful to her. But Angie's Ken was a different proposition. He was quite a good-looking man and women might be tempted to jump into bed with him given the chance. She was wondering what Ken was like in bed when Paul came into the room.

'I thought I could smell coffee,' he said.

'I would have made you one but I heard you on the phone to a client and didn't want to interrupt. Go and sit down and I'll make you one now.'

He sat while she started making it. 'How's it going with your wealthy new client?' she asked.

'OK. All I've got to do is find something that will make her even wealthier.'

'Is she *that* rich?'

'Oh yes. Her husband left her everything, so she won't have to worry about money again.'

'A bit like Fiona then. I bet she'll be set for life once Reggie's will is cleared,' she said, giving him a mug of coffee.

'That depends.'

'Depends on what?' she asked as she sat down again.

'Well, on several things. How much he left and whether it was to be shared with anyone else. Then there's tax et cetera.'

'How do you mean "shared"? He didn't have any other family, did he?'

'A recipient doesn't have to be family. He could have left something to one or more of his women friends or anyone else.'

'Oh, I can't see Fiona standing for that, Paul.'

'Well, Reggie's will isn't my problem so let's drop the subject, shall we?' he said and started drinking his coffee.

After a few moments, Sheila said, 'Did I tell you who Angie thinks might have killed Reggie?'

He screwed up his face in anticipation and said, 'No. But I bet you're going to.'

'She thinks that the police haven't wanted to interview all of us again because they know who did it but need the proof. And that's why there's a policewoman staying there, because the real murderer is the last person anyone would suspect.'

He put his cup down and gave a heavy sigh. 'All right, Sheila. Who is it?'

'Fiona.'

'Fiona!' he said. 'Is Angie mad?'

'Now before you say anything, think about it. She's the one person nobody suspects because they all feel sorry for her. But she had every reason to kill him, the way he's been going to bed with other women. And even if she didn't actually kill him herself, she could have got someone to do it for her. Like that man from the past who was fussing round her like a bee round a honey pot, for instance. Edward whatever his name is.'

Paul listened to her, then finished his coffee and got up without saying anything.

'Well, Paul? What do you think?' she asked, obviously hoping to continue the conversation.

'I think Angie must be very careful who she confides her idea to. If she isn't, she could end up in trouble. And that goes for you as well. Defamation of character is a serious offence, my love.'

'Don't be silly, Paul. It's just us girls enjoying a bit of gossip. Not a case for the Old Bailey.'

Paul left her washing the coffee mugs and returned to his office.

The coroner started the opening inquest on time and was very brief. Once Fiona had confirmed her husband's name and date of birth, he issued the certificate for her to go ahead with the funeral. The pathologist had sent a letter with the details of his findings and this was accepted. Fiona was happy that she was now able to get the funeral over with and move on.

Bill stood holding the passenger door open for Fiona and once she was safely in her seat he started to drive away. His phone rang and he could see that Marsh was his caller.

'Yes, Marsh.'

'I've just had Mandy Lucas on the line. She's received a call from East Ham hospital to tell her that Tony Farrow is in their intensive care unit. He's been run over by a car.'

Bill's reaction was that of disbelief. 'When was this?'

'It happened about two hours ago apparently. The police were called but it seems to have been a hit and run. The witnesses reported that it was a white car. Some thought it was driven by a man but others said it was a woman.'

'Get on to our lads at East Ham. Tell them we have a murder enquiry and that Farrow's accident might be tied in with it. Why did they phone Mandy of all people?'

'Her phone number was the first one in his mobile that they were able to get an answer from.'

Bill thought for a moment, 'See if you can get his mobile brought over to Stafford House. There might be something on it that would be helpful to us. I'm on my way there now but I'm going to call in to see Kate first, so I'll see you later.' He rang off and said to Fiona, 'Sorry about that, ma'am.'

'Are all your days like this?' she asked.

'They vary. Well, the inquest was short and sweet. I hope you feel happier now that you can go ahead with the funeral.'

'It will certainly be a big relief to get it over with. Thank you for taking me this morning, Inspector.'

'It's my pleasure, ma'am. Oh, and while I think of it, I want to ask you a question about last Saturday evening,'

'Yes, Inspector?'

'When you were in the downstairs cloakroom with Edward King, did you have the door partly open or was it shut tight?'

Fiona thought for a moment before answering, 'I think it was shut tight. Why do you ask?'

'I believe you thought you heard Mrs Romaine walk across the hall just before you heard her scream?'

Bill caught a glimpse of her reaction in the mirror and the question appeared to catch her off guard.

'I assumed it was Mrs Romaine. I mean, who else would it have been, coming from the kitchen?'

Bill smiled and gave a casual shrug. 'Yes, of course. As you say, who else?'

Fiona made no further comment on the subject but was very curious as to why the inspector queried her story regarding what she thought Mrs Romaine's movements in the hall were on Saturday evening.

Bill's car phone rang and he quickly answered it. 'Hello?'

'Sergeant Cooper here, sir.'

'Yes, Cooper?'

'I have Edward King on the line, sir. Shall I put him through?'

'Yes, do.' Bill wondered what King would be calling for.

Edward sounded anxious. 'I rang Fiona at home and was told she was with you. Is she all right?'

'Yes. We've just been to the opening inquest and I am driving her back to Stafford House. Why don't you pop over and see her, Mr King?'

Fiona was surprised and quietly asked, 'Edward?'

Bill gave an affirmative nod as King continued, 'I didn't think you wanted me to be seen there until you had the killer in custody.'

'I don't think she will be in any danger with me and our Constable Hamilton there, sir. Come over if you want to. But only if you have the time, of course.'

'I shall make time, Inspector. Thank you.'

'I look forward to seeing you, sir.' Bill hung up and turned to Fiona. 'He appeared to be worried about you not being at home when he was told you were with me.'

'But I told him you would be taking me to the inquest this morning. He's probably got a lot on his mind with his new job and must have forgotten,' Fiona said.

'Yes, that's probably it,' Bill agreed. He then made his way to the hospital to see Kate Weston.

Jessop Ward was the main one for women and Bill was pleased to learn from the sister that Kate was doing fine after her operation. Although Kate had not come round from the anaesthetic, Bill was happy that the operation had been straightforward and that Kate was being looked after by the nurses. After giving Kate's suitcase to the sister, Bill told Constable Markham to stay until Kate regained consciousness and then report back.

Bill went to his car and after telling Fiona of Kate's progress, set off for Stafford House.

The journey from the hospital to Stafford House was taking longer than he wanted because of the busy traffic. When they finally got to the house, Bill was pleased to see that Marsh had arrived and wondered if he had been able to get hold of Tony Farrow's mobile phone. Or at least get the police at East Ham to tell him what calls were on it.

Surprised at seeing the white car in her drive, Fiona said, 'That's David's car. I do hope he isn't going to keep fussing about my health every day.'

'I asked him to call in after his surgery if he could. There's something I need to ask him,' Bill explained.

'Are you not feeling well, Inspector?' asked Fiona.

Touched by her concern, he said, 'I'm fine, ma'am. I need to ask him something about Saturday evening. Just a medical query, that's all.'

He parked his car and went round to the passenger door and helped Fiona out. He then checked his pocket to make sure he still had Farrow's photo with him. Fiona opened the front door with her key and they went into the house.

As they closed the front door, Sally appeared from the

living room and crossed the hall to Bill. 'Did you manage to see Kate, sir?'

'Yes. And she appears to be doing well. Where's Sergeant Marsh?'

'He's in the living room with Doctor and Mrs Wilson.'

'Ask him to join me in the television room. And tell the doctor I shall be with him in a minute.'

'Right, sir.'

As Sally went to leave, Fiona asked, 'Where is Mrs Romaine?'

'In the kitchen, I think, ma'am.'

'Thank you,' said Fiona, and made her way to the kitchen.

In the television room, Bill was feeling confident that he was getting closer to the identity of Sir Reginald's murderer. But he needed to tie up some loose ends before he could be certain. He was going over the case in his mind when Marsh came in and closed the door behind him.

'Did you get Farrow's mobile?' Bill asked.

'They wouldn't let it out of their hands just yet. But they read out the numbers he had on it. The only one I could see that was of interest to us was the one for Mandy Lucas.'

'No calls to Stafford House?'

'No and just one other local number. I've written it down.'

'So if he phoned here, he must have only called Sir Reginald's mobile number.'

'It looks that way, sir.'

'Well, if it wasn't Farrow, I wonder who it was that Lady Fiona said she heard on the telephone extension making that threatening call to her husband?'

'No idea. When she went through the people on his voice-mail with Kate Weston, she said she didn't recognize anyone.'

'Well, never mind that for a moment. Ask Mrs Romaine if she would come and see me. She's in the kitchen,' said Bill.

As Marsh went, Bill hoped his intuition was right and that he would soon be able to wrap this case up. He knew that his reputation of being a successful police officer was at stake. And the last thing he wanted now was to make any mistakes. He was deep in thought when Marsh opened the door and ushered the housekeeper in.

'You wanted to see me, Inspector?' she asked.

Bill gave her a friendly smile and said, 'Yes, Mrs Romaine. As you know, you helped me with my experiment earlier. I am referring to when I asked you to walk across the hallway while I was shut in the downstairs cloakroom. Do you recall?'

'Yes, of course.'

'Well, on Saturday evening were you wearing the shoes you have on now?'

'Oh no, Inspector. These are my everyday shoes. But on an evening when we have guests for dinner or for a special occasion, I always wear a better pair.'

'With leather soles and heels, you mean?' he asked.

His fascination with her shoes was beginning to confuse her. 'Yes. Is it important?'

'Good heavens, no,' he laughed. 'It was just that I couldn't hear you clearly when I was in the cloakroom and began to wonder if my hearing was becoming impaired. Thank you for putting my mind at rest. I don't think a police officer with a hearing aid is an image the commissioner would tolerate.' He smiled.

She looked relieved and said, 'Will there be anything else, sir?'

'Nothing I can think of at the moment, thank you.' Marsh opened the door for her and as she was about to leave, Bill said, 'Oh, on Saturday, did you change your shoes here or at home before you came?'

'I put them on at home before I left. Why do you ask?'

'Just idle curiosity,' Bill said with a smile.

When she was gone, Marsh said, 'You really have got a thing about the shoes, haven't you? It looks like it *was* her that Lady Fiona heard crossing the hall and not the mysterious Mr Farrow.'

'The first thing to do when you have a gut feeling about something is see if you are right. And then if you're not, you eliminate it from your mind,' Bill explained. 'By the way, I ran a check on Mrs Romaine. Her Christian name is Margaret, and she has no children. Her husband was a taxi driver who died from a heart attack and she had an elder sister who died not long ago.'

'When did you find all this out?' asked Marsh.

'This morning. It gave me something to do while you were still in bed. Edward King hasn't arrived, I take it?'

'No. Are you expecting him?'

'Oh yes. He'll be along, you can bank on it.'

'Why would he come here in broad daylight?'

'Because I suggested that he should call in this morning if he had the time.'

Marsh had a puzzled expression and said, 'But you were the one who told him to avoid being seen when he came here.'

'Yes. But that was before I could be absolutely certain he wasn't involved in any way with Sir Reginald's death. And now that I've had time to go over things in more detail, I'm certain that the killer could have only been one of three people. Let me explain.'

He outlined his reasoning and Marsh agreed with him. 'That is exactly the conclusion I came to. And any one of them could have got into Philippa Pane's apartment and killed her.' Before he could continue, his mobile rang. 'DS Marsh.'

'It's Sergeant Pollard here from East Ham. I'm afraid Farrow didn't make it. He died half an hour ago. We found a letter in his wallet that might be of interest in your murder enquiry, so I'm faxing it through to you.'

'Thanks.' He rang off and told Bill what Pollard had said.

'Ring Cooper on the front desk and tell him I want a PC from uniform to bring that fax here as soon as it arrives.'

'Right.' Marsh made the call to Sergeant Cooper.

'Bad luck about Farrow,' said Bill. 'We both had him down as our number one suspect. Never mind. That still leaves us two suspects. And with a bit of luck, we shall soon get that down to just one.' The front doorbell rang and Bill Forward looked at his watch. 'That might be Mr King. I want that fax here before we make our way to the living room. I imagine one of them will be feeling rather nervous by now.'

As Marsh looked into the hall and saw Fiona close the front door and go to the living room with Edward, Mrs Romaine was carrying a tray of coffee from the kitchen to the living room. Bill followed the tantalizing aroma, and diverted Mrs Romaine to leave a cup with him, which he savoured as he walked back to the television room. He didn't have long to wait for the PC to arrive with the fax. After quickly reading it, he gave it to Marsh and told the constable to wait. Then he and Marsh joined the others in the living room.

'My wife said you wanted to ask me a medical question,' said Doctor Wilson. 'Is it one that you couldn't ask on the phone? I do have a busy day ahead of me, Inspector,' he said sharply.

'I'm sorry, Doctor. Her ladyship gave me to understand that you called here every day to check on her progress. I thought it would be better to speak to you here while you were doing so rather than bother you at home or take up valuable time in your surgery. My apologies.'

David Wilson looked slightly uncomfortable as he said, 'No apologies necessary, Inspector. What did you want to ask me?'

'When you were called to examine Sir Reginald on Saturday, how did you establish that he was dead?'

'I felt his pulse. But it was obvious to the trained eye that he was no longer alive.'

'Which pulse did you go to, his neck or his wrist?'

'His neck,' David Wilson replied.

'Bearing in mind that there had been a log fire burning in the study, when you placed your hand on his neck was it normal temperature for a man that had just been killed?'

David Wilson frowned and said thoughtfully, 'As far as I can remember, it was fairly normal.'

Bill gave one of his friendly smiles and said, 'Thank you.'

'Will this take long?' asked David.

Sara Wilson was praying that the inspector would keep his promise and not mention her relationship with Sir Reginald.

'I hope to finish here soon, Doctor,' said Bill. He looked at Fiona. 'My lady, I need to go over some questions in order to clarify certain things. For instance, I was in the cloakroom earlier with the door shut. But I couldn't hear Mrs Romaine clearly enough to know whether she came from the kitchen or not. So perhaps it *was* somebody else that you heard. Someone you naturally assumed was your housekeeper.'

She seemed puzzled by the possibility. 'But if it wasn't her then who would be coming from the kitchen? Everyone else had gone upstairs, apart from Edward and Mrs Romaine. It was she who discovered my husband in the study. So it *must* have been her that I heard coming from the kitchen.'

'I was there too and heard Mrs Romaine walking across the hall, Inspector,' Edward said.

'But is there not one other person who might have entered the house, via the back door?' asked Marsh.

Fiona was intrigued by his question. 'Who would that be?'

'The man Mrs Romaine let in to read the meter on

Saturday. The man who told her he was from the electric company and was left alone in the cloakroom. The same man the company had no knowledge of when I enquired about him,' said Bill.

'But how could he have got in here on Saturday evening, kill my husband, and leave without being seen by anyone?' Fiona shook her head and said, 'I'm sorry, Inspector. I simply cannot believe that someone could do that. It would be far too risky.'

Bill took Farrow's photograph from his pocket and gave it to Fiona and Edward. 'Have either of you ever seen this man before?'

Fiona and Edward were sitting next to each other and both shook their heads.

Mrs Romaine was sitting in a nearby armchair and Bill passed the photograph to her.

'I know you've seen this before but I would like you to have another careful look for me in case you remember him.'

She studied the photograph and said, 'This wasn't the man who came to read the meter. As I've already told you, I've never seen this man before.'

'Who is that man?' asked Fiona.

'He was blackmailing your husband, my lady. His name was Tony Farrow.'

Mrs Romaine was watching Fiona's reaction with interest.

'What do you mean, blackmailing my husband?'

'He recently learned that your husband was his father.'

'Reginald had a son! I don't believe you,' said Fiona.

'Oh, it's true, my lady,' said Marsh. 'Your husband paid to have the child aborted but the boy's mother took him to Social Services to be adopted and kept the money. The couple that adopted him christened him Anthony, but recently the young man received a letter from his natural mother, who

215

was dying. She told him his father's name and the date of his adoption. That's when he decided to blackmail your husband and get paid for his silence. On his birth certificate it just said "father unknown".'

'So who was this man's mother?' asked David Wilson.

'She was also down on the birth certificate as unknown. The mother took the child to Social Services and told them she had found the baby abandoned in a doorway. There was a note which said, "Please take care of my son." The woman refused to give her name and simply ran off. Despite efforts to trace her, she was never found. But she was paid money to have an abortion and keep quiet about the baby. Unfortunately for Sir Reginald, she kept the money and had the child.

'Before she died, a few weeks ago, she wrote to the boy after tracing his foster parents through a private investigator,' continued Bill. 'Anthony was twenty-four years old and would have received his mother's letter around the time your sister died. Isn't that so, Mrs Romaine?' Bill could see his question had surprised her.

'I really don't see what my dear sister's death has to do with all this,' she said, adopting an innocent expression.

'I shall explain the reason for my question. But first I would like you to confirm the phone number at your apartment.' Bill gave a nod to Marsh, who read from his notebook. 'Double seven, double three, five six. Is that correct?'

With everyone staring at her, she was starting to shake. 'Yes, that's my number. I'm in the telephone directory so you know it is,' she said with a casual air.

'But we didn't get it from the directory. We got it from Tony Farrow's mobile. Now why do you suppose your number was on there, Mrs Romaine?'

'I can't imagine,' she replied, calmly.

'We know that he contacted your number several times just recently. Now why would he do that?'

Fiona felt sorry for her and tried to come to Mrs Romaine's defence. 'Inspector, have you asked this man why he has her number? It could be for a completely innocent reason.'

'I wish I could ask him, ma'am. Unfortunately Mr Farrow was killed this morning by a hit-and-run driver.'

Mrs Romaine gasped. 'Oh my God!' The colour drained from her cheeks and she became faint. 'Could I have some water, please?'

David Wilson went to her. 'Put your head down for a moment,' he told her.

Edward jumped up. 'I'll get some water.'

Fiona looked confused as she asked, 'What is going on, Inspector?'

'When your housekeeper has regained her composure, I shall continue, ma'am. I hope it will then become clear what actually happened here on Saturday evening. I would ask you all to be patient until then.'

Edward returned with a glass of water and gave it to David, who put it to Mrs Romaine's lips. 'Sip this slowly and keep your head down until you feel better.'

Nobody spoke for a few moments and then she began to sit up. 'I'm sorry about that. I don't know what came over me.'

'It was the news of your nephew's death that shocked you, wasn't it?'

'I don't know what you're talking about. What nephew?'

'The boy your sister gave birth to twenty-four years ago. Who traced him before she died and told him his father was the wealthy property developer, Sir Reginald Pace-Warren. We have a copy of that letter and when Farrow discovered who his real father was he decided to blackmail him. And with your help that's exactly what he did, isn't it?'

'Could I have some more water, please?' Bill gave her the water and she drained the glass. 'I can't think why I'm so thirsty. It must be something I've eaten,' she said.

'Or perhaps you were getting nervous because you know that lying to the police is a serious offence. Like your story of the man who came to read the electric meter. We know there was no such man, so why did you say there was?' Bill hoped she would fall for his bluff and she did.

'All right, I'll tell you the truth.' she said with reluctance. 'Tony wanted to confront his father face to face and asked me to let him into the study without anyone seeing him.'

'So you telephoned him to let him know Sir Reginald was alone in his study.'

'Yes.'

'Was that before or after the guests had arrived?'

'Before. Tony said he intended to get a lot more money from his father. I warned him that Sir Reginald was a dangerous man to threaten. But he wouldn't listen. That must be when he lost his temper and struck Sir Reginald on the head.'

Fiona frowned with disbelief at what she was hearing. She went to speak but Bill held his hand out to stop her and allow Mrs Romaine to continue.

'And then the following day I phoned Tony and told him that Philippa Pane was telling Lady Fiona that she knew who killed Sir Reginald. That must be when he went to her apartment and killed her.'

Bill glanced at Marsh with a look of satisfaction. 'So you must have heard the phone call that Miss Pane made to her ladyship,' said Marsh.

She became flustered as she made her excuse. 'No. I mean, that was because I happened to lift the receiver in the kitchen. I didn't listen on purpose, I would never do that.'

So whose idea was it to put the jack of clubs on Philippa Pane's body?' asked Bill.

'That was Tony.'

'But where did he get the card from?' asked Marsh.

The questions were beginning to show cracks in her mask of innocence. 'I suppose he took it from the pack when he came earlier.'

'But how would he know the jack of clubs was the card to denote the murderer if he wasn't in the game?' asked Marsh.

Aware that everyone was staring at her, she was nervously trying to think of an answer when Bill said, 'Tony Farrow wasn't here as you claim, was he? He was too smart to risk being seen at this house. So it means that either you or her ladyship struck Sir Reginald with the log and killed him. But it wasn't her ladyship, was it? It was you.'

She licked her lips, in an effort to moisten the dryness in her mouth. 'It was self-defence,' she sobbed. 'I told him it was my sister he'd got pregnant all those years before and that she had recently died. He was surprised, but then he looked at me with an interested smirk and said, "Your sister, eh?" then suddenly grabbed me and pulled me onto his lap. He put his hand on my breast and asked if I was as good in bed as she was, and asked if I've enjoyed any sex since my husband died. He kept making suggestive proposals and wouldn't take his hands from me. I begged him to let go but he wouldn't. So I picked up a log and hit him.'

Fiona listened with disbelief. 'He did all this while I was here getting ready for my guests to arrive!'

Mrs Romaine nodded and wiped her eyes. Bill Forward stood looking directly at her. 'Margaret Romaine. I am arresting you for the murder of Reginald Pace-Warren. You do not have to say anything, but it may harm your defence if you do not mention, when questioned, something which you may later rely on in court. Anything you say may be given in evidence. Do you understand?'

She sat looking at the floor and said in a whisper, 'Yes.'

He gave Sally and Marsh the nod to take her out.

'I can't believe it,' said Fiona.

'Neither can I,' said Edward.

'What will happen to her now?' asked David Wilson.

'She will be taken to the police station and examined by the police surgeon. What happens next depends on her mental and physical condition,' Bill explained.

'I would think she'd pass a medical examination, wouldn't she, David?' Sara asked.

'She has just been through a traumatic experience. There's no telling how it might affect her,' he replied. 'May we go now, Inspector?'

'You are all free to leave. Thank you for your patience.'

As Fiona stood up, David said, 'I don't think you should stay in this house any longer. Our offer is still there for you to stay with us, so please consider it.' He and Sara left with Bill.

Edward stood and took Fiona's hand. 'Why don't we stay in a nice hotel for a while?'

Fiona's reply wasn't what Edward expected. 'Yes, I want to stay in a hotel, Edward, but I have to come to terms with what has happened and need to be on my own for a while. Let me see everyone out. I'll ring you in a day or two.'

As she hurried after the others, Edward stood looking quite crestfallen.

Sally got Mrs Romaine into the car that was waiting with the PC. Marsh gave him his instructions and with Sally sitting in the back with the housekeeper, it returned to the police station.

Fiona told the inspector that she would pack Sally's

overnight bag and get it back to her. She waited for Edward to come out and before he could say anything, closed the door and stood looking at the hall. And with her once happy world appearing to collapse around her, started to cry.

It was late afternoon when Bill was told that Mrs Romaine was well enough to be interviewed again. With a solicitor present, he reminded her that she was under arrest and still under caution and questioned her regarding the second murder. Less than two hours later, Bill went to Superintendent Lamb's office.

'You'll be pleased to know I've got a confession for Philippa Pane's murder as well, sir.'

'Good work, Forward. What did she say?'

'She claimed that she overheard a phone call Miss Pane had made, telling Lady Fiona that she knew who had killed Sir Reginald. She panicked and was frightened Miss Pane knew the truth and had to stop her talking. She also admitted that she had put the jack of clubs on Miss Pane's body. Apparently she thought that would throw suspicion on anyone but her.'

'She fooled you at first.'

'She certainly did for quite a while. It's taught me never to trust a woman just because she makes good coffee. And she did make wonderful coffee.'

'You and your coffee,' said Lamb. 'Let me have your written report in the morning.'

'Marsh is working on that now, sir. And by the way, PC Hamilton was a fine replacement for Kate Weston. They should do well. They both deserve to.'

'Do you think they're ready for promotion?'

'Oh yes. I'd highly recommend either of them. They're both a fine example to the force.'

'I'll keep that in mind. Thanks for doing a good job. I just hope Lady Fiona gets her life together again. Are there any further developments regarding her and Edward King that you know of?'

'I've an idea she wants her own space right now. But I'll be surprised if she doesn't throw caution to the wind and settle down with him once her husband's funeral is over.'

'Do you think she'll give up the title?'

'It wouldn't surprise me. Well, I'd better get back and see how Marsh is doing with the report.'

'You get on well with him, don't you?'

'Yes, I do. He's a bright lad and anxious to get on. From now on I shall give him a bit more responsibility. He's going to make a good copper one day.'

Bill left the superintendent and as he walked down the corridor he saw Sally Hamilton carrying her overnight bag.

'Hello, sir. Lady Fiona sent my things round.'

'That was kind of her. You'd better let Sergeant Marsh know you've got them. I'm sure he'll be pleased. Tell him I'll be with him later. I'm just going to have a coffee.' He did a detour from the direction of his office to the canteen so that Marsh and Sally could be alone for a few minutes. He smiled to himself as he wondered what Superintendent Lamb would say if he knew his inspector was enjoying playing cupid.